PATIENT NURSE

Nurse Wendy Curtis has a big problem in the person of Doctor Roger Harley. She fell in love with him at first sight, and they've worked together for two years — but from the start he has treated her like a sister, when all she wants is his love. Wendy becomes desperate to break the deadlock between them. But fate takes a hand, and she can only hope that her life will develop as she desires . . .

PHYLLIS MALLETT

PATIENT NURSE

Complete and Unabridged

LINFORD
Leicester

First published in Great Britain in 1979

First Linford Edition
published 2018

A catalogue record for this book is available
from the British Library.

ISBN 978–1–4448–3545–8

Published by
F. A. Thorpe (Publishing)
Anstey, Leicestershire

Set by Words & Graphics Ltd.
Anstey, Leicestershire
Printed and bound in Great Britain by
T. J. International Ltd., Padstow, Cornwall

This book is printed on acid-free paper

1

Wendy Curtis sighed as she emerged from the Geriatric Ward of the Greenacre General Hospital in Halesborough. Duty was finished for the day, but she felt strangely depressed as she walked through the park on her way to the flat which she shared with her closest friend, Anne Langton, one of the nurses on Maternity.

Perhaps it was because she was on Geriatric, she told herself. It was not pleasant to be working with the elderly, for it seemed to bring home to her that one day she, too, would get old. But the real reason was the fact that Roger was not getting serious about her. He had been working as Medical Registrar for two years now and they had got along fine from the very start, but there had been no developing romance and she had not been aware of the fact until

Anne had pointed it out — but then Anne was her exact opposite, an extrovert who played the field.

Wendy had always been quiet and rather shy, although she managed to conceal that fact, but usually she became tongue-tied when introduced to a strange man, and the passing years — she was now twenty-six — had not cured her.

She tried to cut short the flow of her thoughts, but she still felt uneasy as she continued to Alma Road, where the flat was situated.

Was she really so concerned that her life lacked romance? She was happy enough with Roger Harley, yet their relationship was one of brother and sister rather than sweethearts, and Roger had done no more than hold her hand or walk arm in arm with her. He was predictable and good company, and she had never considered him in a romantic light until Anne had mentioned the fact that there were no natural developments in their friendship.

Wendy turned into Alma Road. Another sigh escaped her as she paused at a green door and opened her handbag to find her key. Anne was on afternoon and evening duty and their flat would be empty. Wendy was relieved, for life was hectic with Anne around and she felt the need to relax. She had been at the beck and call of Sister Meredith and the patients all morning and felt dead upon her feet.

As she prepared to settle down for the afternoon, Wendy heard the telephone ring and frowned as she went in answer. It was probably for Anne — one of the girl's many admirers who had forgotten which shift she was on — but it was Roger at the other end of the line.

'Wendy — I was hoping you'd gone straight home instead of doing some shopping. I'm afraid I'll have to cry off for this evening. You know we've got a new doctor here today. Well, Dr. Vernon has had an emergency crop up which will take him out of town and it wouldn't be fair of me to leave the new man on his own. I'd better stay with him.'

'That's all right, Roger. Don't worry about it. I don't feel like tennis, anyway. After this morning all I'm fit for is putting up my feet.'

'I know how you feel and you have my sympathy, but your promotion to Sister should be coming through any time now, shouldn't it?'

'I haven't heard anything definite yet, but I do know it is in the pipeline,' she replied. 'What's the new doctor's name, Roger?'

'Scott. Alan Scott. He's a great rugger player — almost up to national level.'

Wendy smiled, for Roger was a sports fanatic, and while she liked most sports, she was also a woman and needed love.

'Well, I must rush,' he then added quickly. 'Something of a flap on here at the moment. 'Bye for now.'

'Good-bye,' she responded, and hung up.

For a moment she stood gazing into space. Had she been too patient with Roger? Was there anything at all in Anne's philosophy of love? The girl never lacked for partners and seemed to live a full, romantic life. The worse she treated men the better they seemed to like her.

Despite her declaration of tiredness, Wendy felt an aversion to spending the evening at home welling up in her mind, and she didn't feel so tired after she had showered and changed out of her uniform. She wished Anne was off duty, but if her friend had been free it was likely she would have had someone in trousers chasing after her.

There was a great deal Wendy could have done on her own, but going to the sports centre did not appeal to her, although there would be a number of her friends present. Deep inside she felt an uncharacteristic urge to do something totally different. The awareness surprised her, for she was rarely adventurous, and when she realized that she had every intention of going out she immediately began to make more definite plans.

The restlessness which had been creeping up on her for weeks seemed to have reached a critical point, and she knew that she just had to do something different or explode. Her parents lived too far away for her to visit — a ninety-mile round trip by road — and she did not possess a car.

She sat down on the sofa and picked up a magazine. She would wait until after tea before venturing out, but an excursion was in order and she began to look forward to it, her mind refusing to concentrate upon the written words on the page before her . . .

The next thing she remembered was waking up with a start, her neck cramped by the awkward position into which she had fallen. For some moments she could not collect her wits, and wondered what time of the day it was. When she looked at the clock on the bookshelf she was surprised to see it registering almost seven and started to her feet, suddenly aware that the telephone was ringing and its shrill sound had startled her out of a deep sleep.

She staggered slightly as she went across to the offending instrument, and moistened her lips before speaking. Then Anne's voice sounded in her ear.

'Wendy, darling, am I glad you're there! Listen, I've made a dreadful faux pas. Derek will be calling for me at seven-thirty and I wasn't able to change duties with Maisie. Now, he is important to me, Wendy, so I want you to do me a favour. Are you seeing Roger tonight?'

'No, but by the tone of your voice I'd guess that if I was seeing him you'd ask me to cancel,' retorted Wendy. 'What kind of a fix are you in now?'

'It's nothing, really, but I don't want Derek to think that I've deliberately stood him up. He's a very promising prospect and I want to see more of him.'

'What's his full name and who is he?' cut in Wendy, stifling a yawn.

'Derek Morley, and his father owns that big garage in Barndale Street. I met him last week and twice I've had to cut a date with him.'

'What do you want me to tell him exactly? Anything but the truth, I suspect.'

'Actually, you can tell him the truth this time,' Anne replied. 'I really forgot about the arrangement and when I mentioned it to Maisie she said it was too late to put through.'

'All right. You don't get off duty until ten. I haven't got to be hospitable to him until then, have I?'

'I'll be your friend for life if you would, but, knowing you, I think he'd take flight long before then. I wouldn't trust him with anyone else, but you're such a stick-in-the-mud that I can trust him with you. Let him down easily, Wendy, there's a good girl. Now I must rush. I've got to get back on duty. See you later.'

'Good-bye.' Wendy sighed as she went to check her make-up and general appearance. It was a bore having to see one of Anne's innumerable boy-friends, and she had planned to go out herself.

When the doorbell rang some thirty minutes later she was resigned to the situation and hurried to open the door.

The man standing outside was tall and broad-shouldered, in his early thirties, with blue eyes and fair, wavy hair.

'Hello,' he said. 'You must be Wendy.' His smile was genuine and attractive.

'You're very well informed,' she answered. 'And you're Derek, obviously.'

'Someone is imparting a great deal of information,' he countered. 'Is Anne ready, or is she going to keep me waiting half the evening?'

'I'm afraid it will be longer than half the evening. She doesn't get off duty until ten.'

'But we had a date!'

'She told me, and asked me to apologise. Nurses often work very

9

unsociable hours and to minimize the inconvenience it is sometimes possible to change duties with a colleague. She had this evening set up for a swop, but it fell through.'

'I see.' He shook his head, his blue eyes gleaming. She was aware that he was subjecting her to a close scrutiny. 'Well, I'm not going to wait in for her. You look as if you're all ready to go out. I expect you've been waiting around for me to call in order to give me the brush-off.'

'No. I've been waiting for you to call, but not to fob you off. Anne is really upset over this and she wants to see you again.'

'Then why didn't she ask you to stand in for her? You're her closest friend, aren't you?'

'She has been telling you a lot.'

'Well you've got to be close, sharing a flat with her. You're the one who has a doctor as a boy-friend, aren't you?'

'I wouldn't call him a boy-friend. We're just friends.' Wendy was aware of a sinking sensation in her stomach as she spoke. Why hadn't Roger treated her like a normal girl? Why hadn't he ever kissed her romantically? He had pecked her on the cheek once or twice and kissed her forehead, but he had never seized her with passion and she was beginning to wonder if there was something wrong with her. She noticed that he was smiling, and asked quickly: 'Do you think that's impossible in this day and age?'

'Certainly not, but a beautiful girl like you deserves something more than a friend.'

'Flattery won't wash with me,' she retorted.

'I don't have to flatter you,' he replied. 'Anne is my girl. But where are you going this evening? It's been wasted for me. Can I take you out somewhere?'

'And what do you think Anne would say about that?'

'There wouldn't be anything in it,' he remarked. 'Either that or I waste an evening.'

'Is your time so precious? What's one evening?'

'Hey, keep talking like that and I'll begin to understand why that doctor friend is only a friend! Now what about it? I have a new car I want to run in and I know a dozen girls who would jump at the chance to be the first to sit in that passenger seat.'

'Then I suggest that you go and pick one of them up,' she murmured.

'All right. Give Anne a message for me, will you? Tell her I'll call some time.'

'I hope I haven't scared you off,' Wendy said. 'Anne thinks a great deal of you.'

'I think a lot of that girl, too. See you around.'

She nodded and stepped backwards as he turned away. For a moment she watched him, then she went into the house and closed the door.

There would never be a dull moment with a man like Derek Morley around, she told herself. He would certainly seize her and kiss her at the first opportunity. The depression which seemed to have dug its claws into her was biting now and she stifled a sigh, fetched her handbag, and let herself out of the house. She needed some fresh air and there was nothing better than a long walk to blow away the cobwebs in the mind.

Wendy found herself going in the direction of the hospital, so she entered the park and sat down upon a bench.

Two nurses came by, out for a stroll, and they paused to chat with Wendy.

'Not on your own again?' asked Linda Gale, who worked in Women's Medical. 'This is Marj Blake, who started with us today. Marj, this is Wendy Curtis.'

'Hello,' Marj said, smiling. 'I've heard about you, Wendy.'

'I hope it wasn't bad,' Wendy answered. 'How are you, Marj? Think you'll like working at Greenacre?'

'Yes. I've found one hospital is much like another — the only real difference is the people who work in it, and Greenacre seems to have a good staff.'

'We can't grumble, by and large,' Linda broke in. 'Why are you sitting here, Wendy? Are you waiting for someone?'

'No. Roger was held up at the hospital so I'm out for a breath of fresh air.'

'It's all right so long as you're not here when it gets dark,' Linda commented. 'Care to join us? It will be better than staying on your own.'

'Thanks. I could do with some company.' Wendy arose and they walked on. 'I felt too tired to go to the sports centre.'

'After a shift at the hospital I don't feel like any strenuous games,' Linda retorted. 'I've been there as a spectator and I've seen you and Roger playing, but I'd rather watch than take part.'

'You'll have to show me around there one evening,' said Marj. 'I'm rather keen on sport. I like tennis, squash and swimming. Once I settle in I'll have to look around for a partner.'

'We've got a number of fanatics on the staff,' Linda replied. 'I don't think you'll have trouble finding anybody.'

Wendy enjoyed the stroll and they ended up in the café near the hospital, which was a favourite haunt of the staff when they were off duty. Wendy was surprised to see Roger at a table with Sister Gilbert and a stranger. Roger looked up and a smile came to his face when he saw her. She saw him speak to his companions, then come towards her, and she excused herself from her company and joined him.

'Hello. I didn't expect to see you in here.' Roger Harley took her hands for a moment. He was a good-looking man in all respects, with a high forehead and a strong chin. His nose was straight, his eyes steady, and Wendy felt a pang of longing stab through her.

'I decided to go out for a walk,' she explained. 'Are you off duty?'

'No. We had a breathing space and I've left word where I can be found. I decided to bring the new man over to show him where everyone meets. Come, I'll introduce you.'

Wendy followed him across to the table. Roger made the introductions and Wendy found herself shaking hands with Alan Scott.

'Hello, Wendy,' he said softly. 'Roger has been telling me about you. I hear that you swing a mean racket!'

'Hello,' she responded, smiling. 'Is that a compliment, I wonder?'

'I'd say so, the way Roger spoke.' There was a gentleness in Alan's tones which sent a thrill along Wendy's spine. There was admiration in his eyes and she knew a longing deep within which sprang from a desire to find romance.

'I'll have to give you a game one of these evenings,' she replied, 'and then you can judge for yourself.'

'Yes,' said Roger enthusiastically, 'that's a good idea. There are times when we can't get away together, Wendy, and I know you don't like being on your own. After this evening, Alan and I will be on duty at different times, and it would be a good idea if you took him in hand a bit, just until he settles down here.'

'That sounds like a good idea to me,' put in Alan, his eyes fixed upon Wendy's face.

'Well, we have to be getting back to the hospital,' Roger went on. 'See you tomorrow, Wendy.'

Wendy returned to the table where Linda and Marj were seated. Alan Scott turned in the doorway as he followed Roger out and glanced in her direction and she knew his interest in her was very real — but what really shocked her was the fact that she welcomed that interest, and wondered just what was happening to bring about such a drastic change in her attitude.

★   ★   ★

Next morning when she went on duty, Wendy learnt that two of her elderly patients were showing signs of deterioration. She felt further depressed by the news, and realized that she would have to make an effort to be more objective in her approach to the ward.

Alan Scott appeared on the round, and when he saw Wendy he left Sister Meredith and approached her, a smile upon his face. He seemed a cheerful sort, and she had heard his voice echoing out along the ward as he greeted each patient.

'Good morning, Nurse,' he said. 'You're looking a bit down. Is anything wrong?'

Wendy explained her feelings and saw his nod of sympathy.

'This is the sad part of our work,' he agreed. 'Nobody likes to think that age is always creeping up on us. I understand how you feel, but if you look at it in the light that whatever you do here is helping them then you ought to feel easier.'

'Yes, I know. It's just that I've always felt that this is the saddest ward in the hospital.'

'Now I feel that way about Children's,' he countered. 'I hate to see children suffering.'

Wendy nodded, but said nothing. They were always closer to reality in this job and she ought to have become accustomed to the fact by now. But she was aware that part of her problem stemmed from her dissatisfaction with her personal life.

'I must get on,' Alan said, breaking into her thoughts. 'Will you be going to the sports centre this evening?'

'I don't know. Roger is on duty. He should have been off last evening.'

'I know. He stayed on to show me the ropes and I appreciate that, especially after meeting you and seeing what a sacrifice he made.'

'There's nothing serious between us,' Wendy said hastily. 'I know it must sound trite, but Roger and I are just good friends.'

He smiled, his eyes sparkling. 'Roger told me. I warned him last night that someone might come along and steal you from him, but he said he didn't want to tie you down.'

She returned his smile, but his words about Roger's attitude did not reassure her. When he departed to continue his round she went to work with grim determination. There was so much to do and they were understaffed, as usual.

After Doctor's Round, the work of the ward went on, and Wendy found herself in charge of Mrs. Andrews, a lady of seventy-four years, who had no relations except a distant cousin. When Wendy approached her the old lady seemed in fairly high spirits.

At that moment Roger entered the ward.

'How are you today, Mrs. Andrews?' he asked.

'Fine, Doctor. I'll be going home next week.'

'If you continue to make progress,' he said. Then he transferred his attention to Wendy. 'I just dropped by to have a word with you,' he went on. 'Have you seen Alan Scott this morning?'

'Yes. He's just finished his round in here.'

'Did he ask you to play tennis with him this evening?'

'No. We did pass the time of day, but nothing definite was said.'

'Perhaps he's a bit shy. I'll tell him that I mentioned it to you, and if he is keen then he can come and tell you what time he can pick you up. He's got a car.'

'Well, I don't know!' Wendy was critical of the suggestion. If Roger thought anything at all of her he wouldn't want another man to take her out. 'But if he'd like me to show him around, then I'll do so.'

'Good. It might do you good to have a change of company. Now I must dash. I have to be in Men's Medical in five minutes, and there's some coffee waiting for me in my office.'

She watched him depart and then shook her head as she returned her attention to her patient, but Mrs.

Andrews was looking at her with a speculative light in her eyes.

'You are involved with Dr. Harley,' she observed.

'Not really.'

'But you'd like to be, is that it? Doesn't he pay enough attention to you?'

'We play tennis together and go for walks, but we've never been serious. I like Dr. Harley and he likes me.'

'But you don't strike sparks together, is that it? You're certainly concerned about it, I can tell.'

'I hope it doesn't show too clearly,' Wendy murmured. 'Come along, I'll see you safely into the day-room.'

They walked together into the large lounge which served the patients as a day lounge, and when she had settled Mrs. Andrews into an easy-chair, Wendy went to the office, and waited while Sister Meredith used the telephone. When her superior put down the receiver she turned to Wendy.

'There are two more admissions on

their way in,' she said. 'By the way, I've been meaning to talk to you for a couple of days now, but never seem to get the time. Is anything wrong? You haven't been looking your usual pleasant self.'

'Do you mean that I've been going round with a long face?'

'No, but I know you pretty well and I can usually tell when someone is worrying about something. Any problems bothering you?'

Wendy paused and moistened her lips. 'You do know that I'm not really happy working in this department, don't you?'

'Ah!' Sister Meredith smiled sympathetically. 'Is that all that's bothering you? Well, don't worry. You'll get used to it, although, from all accounts, you'll be leaving me in the near future. Your promotion is on the cards. But I understand how you feel, Nurse. Stick it out, and I promise you that it won't be for much longer.'

Wendy nodded and went back to

work, lost in thought, and when lunch arrived she went into the kitchen to help with the special diets. After lunch Alan Scott entered the ward and approached her. There was a smile on his lips, but he seemed slightly ill at ease.

'I have had word from Roger that you'd like a game of tennis tonight,' he said. 'Roger is on duty so I've stepped into the breach and I place myself at your service.'

'That's very kind of you!' Wendy exclaimed. 'Roger did mention it. Have you found your way around yet?'

'Frankly, no!' His smile was captivating, but he had a challenging manner, an intangible ability to elate her which came from his personality. 'Though Roger described how I could find your flat and I expect you to take it from there.'

'Fine. I'll expect you to call for me then.'

'My pleasure. At what time?'

'Seven? Unless you finish rather late.'

'Seven will be fine, but keep an eye out for me just in case I run into any difficulties finding your flat.'

'All right.' Wendy grinned, and when he had departed she discovered that her spirits had risen considerably. She went about her duties with a lighter heart.

⋆　⋆　⋆

Going off duty early in the afternoon, she walked homeward with more spring in her step than she had experienced for some time, and the self-doubting questions that had been invading her mind for weeks were strangely absent. She spent the afternoon relaxing, and checking her tennis gear, and before seven was awaiting Alan Scott's arrival with anticipation. The front door slammed and her heart seemed to lurch, but when the sitting-room door opened it was Anne who appeared, and her flat-mate and best friend paused and gazed at her in some astonishment.

'Not tennis this evening, surely!'

Anne cried, coming into the room. 'I heard that Roger is on duty.'

'That's right. I'm going with Alan Scott, the new doctor.'

'You're what?' Anne shook her head in wonder. 'Are you serious?'

'Yes, I am — and I don't know whether to be pleased or not. I can't understand why Roger would be prepared to throw me into the arms of another man.'

'By the sound of your voice you won't be disappointed if that happened,' came the observant retort. 'I've noticed that you haven't been yourself lately. What's the trouble? Are you and Roger falling out?'

'As far as I know we've never been more than tennis partners.'

'And that's beginning to worry you, eh?' Anne chuckled. 'Good for you, Wendy. I've been saying for a long time that you and Roger are not suited. It's all right for you to play tennis with him and let him come the big brother act with you, but there's more to life than that, you know.'

'Yes, I am aware of the fact, having watched you over the past months,' Wendy countered, 'but this evening's excursion is nothing to concern yourself about. I'm only a tennis partner being loaned to a friend.'

'You're like a doormat!' Anne exclaimed. 'I'll never understand why you let Roger treat you as he does. You should have come to a firm understanding with him months ago.'

'What kind of an understanding?'

'You two don't act like lovers!'

'We're not lovers! Roger hasn't even kissed me seriously.'

'What? You've got to be kidding!'

'I wish I was.' Wendy shook her head. 'I'm beginning to get a complex about myself. There must be something wrong with me.'

'What you need is a change. Roger just takes you for granted. I told you that a long time ago. But you've not been yourself lately, so I spoke to Sister Meredith after you came off duty this afternoon and she told me what's troubling you. How would you care to change duties with me? I've been transferred to Women's Surgical as from tomorrow and you know I detest that. I'd rather do Geriatric, if you'd agree. They're talking about making you a Sister and putting you into Surgical, so it's obvious that you'll be more suited to it.'

'Oh, Anne, would you change?'

'I'm asking you to, aren't I? What about it? Is it a deal? If it is I'll call the hospital now and confirm it. I've already had the change pencilled in because I thought you'd jump at the chance.'

'I'll swop with you. It will be one problem less for me to face. I don't know what's wrong with me, but I've been unsettled ever since I went into Geriatric.'

'Don't worry about it. You're too sensitive, that's your trouble. You'll get along fine in Surgical, and as I don't like that you're not doing yourself any favours, you're helping me out.' Anne went back into the hall and made a telephone call, and Wendy breathed deeply, filled with relief. 'That's settled, then,' continued Anne, returning and closing the door. 'You'll report to Sister Gilbert in Women's Surgical in the morning. I'll take your place with Sister Meredith. Now what about this other problem you've got?'

'What's that?'

'Roger. Are you in love with him?'

'I don't know — and that's the truth. I don't feel as if I am.'

'Heavens! You'd know if you were! Would you miss him terribly if he didn't see you again?'

'I expect I would. We've been out together so many times, but it wouldn't be a tragedy if I stopped seeing him — at least, that's the way I feel knowing that I will see him again.'

'Perhaps you won't want to after you've been out with Alan. I've heard that he's a real charmer. Some of the girls are saying that they'd like an evening out with him. I'll tell you one thing — you can test Roger now. If he does have any feelings for you tucked away somewhere inside him then going out with another man should bring it out.'

The doorbell rang before Wendy could protest, and Anne paused and glanced at her watch.

'You'd better answer it,' she went on. 'It won't be for me. I'm not due out for another hour and all my friends are very punctual. That's the way I've trained them. Go on and have a nice time. I'll see you later.'

She turned and walked into her room while Wendy went to answer the door. Wendy opened it to see Alan standing on the step, a smile upon his face. He was dressed in a white T-shirt and shorts.

'Hello,' he said. 'I found the place all right, you see. Are you ready?'

'As ready as I'll ever be,' she responded. 'But won't you feel cold later, when the sun goes down?'

'Don't worry, I've got a sweater in the car. Where's your stuff?'

'In the house. I'll get it.' She went into the sitting-room to collect her equipment and when she returned he took everything from her. She suppressed a sigh as she walked with him to his large grey Jaguar. Roger had always left her to carry her own gear. But times were changing, she thought, and it was up to her to see that the changes were for the better.

2

Wendy enjoyed a marvellous evening. She beat Alan at tennis, although she suspected that he let her win for his form suddenly went from very good to less than average in the last sets. Then they went into the restaurant for long drinks, and she sipped an orange juice and thrilled to the sense of elation which gripped her.

It had all started with Anne offering to change duties with her, and she knew a tremendous burden had been lifted from her mind, but this strange man sitting opposite her was also contributing to her high spirits. He had proved to be a good player and his game was unpredictable, a fact which brought home to her the truth that she had come to know Roger too well.

'I thoroughly enjoyed that,' he suddenly observed. 'When I arrived here I had second thoughts about the wisdom of accepting the post, but now I'm certain I'm going to like it. You play squash, too, I hear. Are you as good at it as you are at tennis?'

'Schoolgirl champion and county player,' came the reply.

'What county would that be? You're not a local girl.'

'I'm not. My parents live about fifty miles from here, but initially we came from Sussex.'

'Are you happy here?' His eyes bored into hers and Wendy felt confused. She could see a network of laughter lines around his eyes and there was a smile upon his lips even now. He always seemed to be smiling and yet there was a sense of seriousness about him.

'Happy?' she echoed.

'You don't seem happy. When I met you last night I said to myself: There's a girl who's not getting the best out of life. Her eyes are proclaiming that she is unfulfilled, or something like that.'

She chuckled despite the pang that

cut through her breast. He nodded approvingly.

'You should smile more often, you know. I think Roger is something of an idiot, don't you? But don't quote me on that — it might be misconstrued.'

'Why should you think he's an idiot? He's a very clever doctor. He and I have been close friends for longer than I care to remember.'

'That's what I mean. He's only a friend. If I had been friends with you as long as he has I wouldn't have let a stranger come along and take you out for the evening. I'd be afraid of losing you.'

'Perhaps he doesn't care if our friendship ends,' Wendy retorted. 'But two people don't have to fall in love just because they happen to share the same interests, do they?'

'Why not? That's how marriages have been made for centuries. Why change the system now? Or are you a career nurse? You are extremely efficient, so I've been told.'

'Have you been asking questions about me?'

'Certainly. I like to know all about the girl I'm spending an evening with.'

'But what about you? Where do you come from and what made you pick Greenacre Hospital?'

'I needed to get away from the position I was holding.' His face was suddenly impassive, his voice husky. 'I'm a bit of a fool, I suppose. I always become involved with the girls I go around with although I never have found the right one, or even one who seems suitable. Perhaps it's me. I don't know.'

He lapsed into silence and Wendy realized that they were becoming closer, more friendly. He was no longer a stranger, although she still hadn't learnt anything of his background. But his anonymity was fading and he was emerging as a person. He had a strong personality which appealed to Wendy, but she fancied that at this moment she would have warmed to anyone. She had reached a crossroads in her life emotionally, and Roger was no longer filling the needs she felt growing inside her.

'I suppose we'd better go,' he then said with a note of regret in his voice. 'When can we come again?'

'I'm off duty every evening this week, but tomorrow I'm going into Women's Surgical.' She shrugged. 'I don't think my shift will change, but you'll have to check with Roger about my evenings. He has first call upon me as a partner.'

'All right.' He smiled as he rose from his chair and collected their gear. 'Come on, I'll drive you home.'

Wendy felt a warm glow as she sat beside Alan in his car. For the first time in months she seemed to be alive.

'Would you care to have a drink with me?' Alan asked as he drew into the kerb outside her flat. 'It's still very early.'

'I'll have to go in and change, but what about you?'

'I've got my clothes on the back seat.

I'll put them on while you get into a dress.'

'All right, but you can come in if you wish.'

'That's okay. I don't want to press my luck too far. It may not please Roger if I really made myself at home in your company.'

'It really has nothing to do with Roger,' she heard herself saying, and was filled with mild surprise at the attitude beginning to form in her mind. There was a streak of animosity, or antipathy, growing against Roger, and she believed that she was subconsciously blaming him for being so disinterested in her as a woman . . .

When she went out to the car, Alan sat behind the wheel as she had left him, but now he was wearing grey trousers and a navy-blue jacket.

'That's better,' he commented. 'Where do we go from here?'

'There's a little pub close to the hospital called The Centurion. That's where most of the staff go.'

'Then let's try it. I'd like to meet as many of them as possible. I'm the gregarious type. The more the merrier so far as I'm concerned.'

Wendy thought of Roger as they drove through the town. Roger seemed to be the exact opposite to Alan. Roger preferred his own company, or just their own when they were together.

Sitting in the crowded pub with a sherry in her hand, listening to Alan talking generally and greeting colleagues occasionally, Wendy realized just how much she had been missing, and by the time the evening came to an end she decided she was making some very drastic changes in her life. Roger would now have to take a less important position. She would not depend so much upon him for company. That might bring him to a more normal outlook, although she doubted it.

Alan drove her home just before eleven, and as he stopped the car outside the flat he turned to her.

'Well, here you are, safe and sound,' he said gently. 'I hope I haven't been too much of a bore. I do run on a bit when I get going.'

'You weren't a bore,' she answered quickly. 'Quite the opposite, in fact. I can't remember when I last enjoyed myself so much. I'm aware that I've been slipping into a rut, but today a number of changes have taken place and I intend to see that I go on following the new course that I've set myself.'

'That sounds interesting. It isn't every day that a woman digs her heels in and takes a fresh look at the way her life is going. But remember one thing, Wendy. When you make changes in your life it doesn't only affect you. Life is like the surface of a pond — someone throws in a stone and everyone feels the ripples.'

Alan took her hand and for a moment she fancied he was about to kiss her, but he merely squeezed it gently and then opened his door. She sat still while he walked around the car to open the door for her, and when she alighted and stood beside him she felt a stab of disappointment, for she would dearly have loved a good-night kiss from him. Then she realized that he was acting the gentleman because she was so closely involved with Roger.

'Here's to the next time,' Alan then said softly. 'Thank you, Wendy. I'll look out for you around Women's Surgical in the morning.'

'Good night,' she murmured, and walked slowly to her door. He waited until she had entered the flat before driving away, and she stood in the hall listening to the sound of the car departing.

When she got into bed she lay for a long time thinking over the events of the evening. Matters were coming to a head despite herself, and she knew she would have to have a long, serious talk with Roger. She heard Anne come in very quietly and go to bed, and then she turned on her side and closed her eyes, forcing her mind to release its grip upon the situation in which she found herself. The next thing she knew, Anne was shaking her shoulders urgently.

'Come on, lazy-bones! If you don't get a move on we're both going to be late.' Anne darted from the room, muttering about burning toast, and Wendy threw aside her bedcovers and hurriedly arose.

Anne had prepared a skimpy break-fast by the time Wendy was dressed in her uniform and ready to face the day. There was no time for conversation. They ate quickly, then left the flat for the hospital. The day was warm, with the sun shining from a clear blue sky, and traffic had not yet started to build up on the streets.

'Well, what kind of an evening did you have?' asked Anne as they passed through the park.

'Quite a nice one,' Wendy replied, and began to narrate the incidents which had taken place. By the time she had explained everything they were entering the hospital, and Anne smiled as their glances met.

'I'm glad you've made friends with Alan Scott,' she said, 'and a bit of competition is good for such likes as Roger Harley. He doesn't know he's alive, but if jealousy bites him then you could be in for a lively time.'

'I don't mean a thing to Roger,' Wendy said wistfully.

'Time will tell. Now you'd better report to Sister Gilbert. You don't want to blot your copybook on your first day in Women's Surgical.'

Wendy went on alone, and realized that she was looking at life from a different viewpoint. She was singing under her breath and her step seemed lighter. When she reached Women's Surgical she saw Sister Gilbert seated at a desk and tapped at the office door.

Sister Gilbert turned and looked at her, a smile coming to her face. 'Good morning, Nurse! I'm very happy to have you with me. Just give me a moment to finish going through the night reports and I'll be with you. You're not joining me as an ordinary nurse. I've been instructed to give you some of my work to handle and you are to begin to learn how to run a surgical ward. Take a walk around the ward and talk to the patients. Staff Nurse Vernon is seeing to the breakfasts. She'll carry on, but you'll help me with the patients due for op's today. I'm looking through the drug sheets and list of Theatre times. When I've got everything organized I'll be with you.'

Wendy made her way round the ward, chatting to patients, listening to complaints and noting details of requests.

Then Sister Gilbert approached, carrying some notes. She called Wendy to one side and spoke in low tones: 'You can take care of these patients this morning, Nurse,' she said. 'Mrs. Brown is first. She's the first of three hysterectomies this morning. Get her ready for Theatre and give her the pre-med. Stick closely to the timetable, unless you hear something to the contrary from me. Mr. Butler is operating today and he's a stickler for punctuality. If he falls behind schedule, even by a few moments, and it's our fault then we can expect trouble, so we want everything running smoothly.'

'Yes, Sister.' Wendy took the notes and scanned them. She was eager to begin work and went to Mrs. Brown's bedside. The woman was calm and collected, although her eyes betrayed some inner apprehension, and Wendy smiled. 'It won't be long now, Mrs. Brown,' she said soothingly. 'You're the first down this morning and it will soon be over. I'll give you a pre-med, which is an injection. You're not afraid of injections, are you?'

'They've never bothered me. I've had three children in my time, but I'll be glad to get this over with.'

Wendy went to prepare the injection, then administered it. Mrs. Brown lay motionless, and Wendy patted the woman's shoulder comfortingly and went on about her duties. Time began to pass. Mrs. Brown was returned from Theatre and replaced in her bed. Wendy prepared a post-operative injection for her, checked the drip that was needed, and stood by while Sister Gilbert checked that everything was right. She was rewarded with a smile and a wink, and began to feel more at home in the ward . . .

When Wendy went to lunch she saw Anne in the dining-room and sat beside her friend.

'Well,' Anne declared, 'no need to ask how you feel about the change. It's written all over your face. I'm glad I went into Geriatric instead of you. You can keep Surgical.'

'Thanks, I will. I've had a good morning, but what about the patients you've been caring for?'

'Don't ask. You don't like working there so don't make any inquiries.' Anne glanced at her watch and sighed. 'I'd better be getting back on duty. See you later, Wendy.'

After Wendy had finished her break she returned to Women's Surgical to find Roger waiting in the office, talking to Sister Gilbert, and Sister arose and gave a little grin.

'You have five minutes before you're due back in the ward, Nurse,' she commented as she departed.

'Thank you, Sister.' Wendy gazed into Roger's dark eyes as she spoke.

'What are you doing this evening?' he asked.

'Nothing in particular. You're off duty, aren't you?'

'Yes. I suggest we go to the sports centre.'

'Sounds interesting,' she commented slowly, and saw a frown come to his face.

'But not interesting enough?' he queried. 'You know, Wendy, I'm beginning to wonder if there isn't something wrong. Have you got something on your mind you'd care to talk about?'

'Yes, there is — but this is neither the time nor the place to discuss it. Look,

Roger, I think I'll stay in tonight. I'll see you on your next evening off, all right?'

Roger stared hard at her for a moment, then he shrugged and said: 'So be it.' He turned and left the office, closing the door quietly behind him.

★ ★ ★

During the next week, Wendy saw Roger during the evenings when he was off duty and Alan on the alternate evenings. But, as time went by, she realized just how much she had come to dislike the past months. Her attitude towards Roger had changed abruptly, and the former easy camaraderie between them seemed artificial now, in her eyes.

Perhaps it was the arrival of Alan in her life, she thought, while considering the situation as she dressed to go out with Alan. He was completely opposite to Roger in every way; Roger could see no further than an evening spent at the sports centre, but Alan had been suggesting that they should give sport a miss for once.

At first Wendy had refused point-blank, because she accepted that Roger was prepared to let her be in Alan's company so long as they went to play tennis or squash, but then she could no longer contain her feelings and saw no reason why she should not go out on a date with Alan.

Now Wendy was filled with anticipation as she awaited Alan's arrival. Anne was off duty and preparing to go out with Derek and she commented upon Wendy's preparations.

'Don't tell me you're going to the sports centre in that!' she declared, when Wendy entered the sitting-room wearing her favourite green dress.

'Of course not. I'm going out to dinner with Alan.'

'My! You're changing a great deal and coming out of your shell. I've been telling you for months that Roger isn't right for you and that you're wasting your time with him, but now you suddenly go overboard for another man.'

'I haven't gone overboard for another man!'

'You must have or you wouldn't snap at your best friend,' retorted Anne in her teasing tone. 'But you're doing only half the right thing, you know.'

'I don't know, so you'd better tell me. What do you mean, only half the right thing?'

'You're doing right by going out with another man, but you've picked the wrong man, by all accounts. Haven't you heard the tales going the rounds about Alan Scott?'

'I never listen to gossip.'

'Then perhaps you should. There's never any smoke without fire. I don't think Alan is the right man for you.'

'You don't think Roger is the right man for me.' Wendy shrugged. 'Have you any idea what type of man I should look for?'

'There are some girls who never seem to be able to get everything right,'

Anne said patiently. 'You seem to be one of them. Roger isn't interested in marriage. You've known it for a long time, but refused to accept it.'

'But who said I was interested in marriage?'

'Well, you're the one who's been moping around here because there's been no romance in your life — but you'll get plenty of romance from Alan, believe me, and it won't be for real. He'll leave you flat as soon as another pretty face takes his eye. That will leave you worse off than you were with Roger.'

'I wish you wouldn't read so much into my life,' Wendy protested. 'I'm not like you, Anne. I don't need all those men in my life.'

'I know that, and that's why I'm saying you should find a decent sort you can settle down with. Your way of life indicates that you're a one-man girl and you have to find Mr. Right before you can be happy. All I'm saying is that Alan isn't the right one for you.'

'You're beginning to kill my anticipation for this evening,' said Wendy. 'I've a good mind to stay in now.'

'Don't be foolish. Go out and have a good time with Alan, but don't put too much store in what he says. Take him at face value and leave it like that. I know what I'm talking about. If you're not careful you're going to be left high and dry, with an almighty large chip on your shoulder.'

The doorbell rang, and Wendy sighed in relief.

'I'll go,' she said. 'It will probably be Alan.'

'Have you got your door key?'

'Yes, but I won't be late.'

'Have a nice time then.' Anne turned and went into her bedroom.

Wendy left the sitting-room and answered the door to find Alan standing there. He looked immaculate, and he whistled softly at the sight of her.

'We'll have to forget about the sports centre more often if you're going to dress like that,' he commented. 'The more I see you the more I wonder what's wrong with Roger.'

'What do you mean, what's wrong with him?' she asked as they walked to his car.

'He isn't serious about you, is he?'

'I'm not serious about him!' Wendy wondered if that statement was exactly true. She had become accustomed to Roger, that was the trouble. They had been together for so long that they knew nothing else and old habits seemed to die hard. But she pushed all thoughts of Roger away as Alan joined her in the car.

Alan certainly proved to be diverting. He took her to dinner in the largest hotel in the town, and was attentive and considerate. He talked or listened intently, and gave Wendy the impression that she was the only girl in the world.

Wendy's most vivid recollection of the evening was that it seemed the most romantic and wonderful she had ever experienced. She seemed encompassed by a warm haze of excitement and anticipation and could only marvel that Alan found her interesting enough to want her company. It had never been like this with Roger and the knowledge of how it had been only served to bring home with more force exactly what she had been missing.

After the meal they sat drinking coffee and Alan asked Wendy about her past — demanding even the smallest details of her history.

'There's nothing very interesting about me,' she remarked carelessly.

'Now don't say that!' he remonstrated. 'I'm not Roger, remember. I'm not likely to take you for granted.'

Her face sobered slightly at the mention of Roger's name and Alan chuckled.

'I touched upon a nerve there, didn't I? I have the feeling that you are going through withdrawal pangs so far as he's concerned. Is that true? He doesn't deserve you, Wendy — and you deserve better than he's given you. He's been wasting your time. Life is flitting by, and if you don't get some fun and excitement while you're young you won't get any when you're older.'

Wendy leaned back in her chair, feeling giddy with the heady wine of excitement, as if she were a schoolgirl out on her first date. Alan seemed to thrill her as she had never been affected before, and when it was finally time for them to leave he escorted her from the hotel as if she were a duchess.

On the drive back to her flat, Wendy sat silent and relaxed in the car, and Alan spoke quietly about the evening.

'I didn't think I'd find someone like you here when I arrived, Wendy. You say that you and Roger don't have an understanding, but I've watched points over the past weeks and I feel you are sincere in your conviction that Roger doesn't mean anything to you. That being the case, I plan to court you and I won't easily be put off.'

Wendy listened to his words with her pulses racing and, when he drew into the kerb around the corner from Alma Road and switched off the engine and lights, she half-turned towards him, aware that he was going to kiss her. She was strangely eager for his embrace and went into his arms as he reached for her. When his lips touched hers she closed her eyes and shuddered with ecstasy. A sense of unreality touched her mind and she felt as she imagined Cinderella must have felt at the Prince's ball. She was tantalized by their contact, and clung to him, gripped by strange forces, the nature of which she could barely begin to comprehend. Her senses whirled and blood coursed wildly through her veins.

At last she felt fulfilled. The nagging uneasiness of weeks had dissipated instantly in the magic of that ardent embrace and she was elated as he moved back from her and started the car.

'Roger is going to find out just how much of a fool he is when we tell him that we're going to start seeing each other. He'll have to find himself another tennis partner.'

'I don't want to hurt Roger,' Wendy said quickly, coming down to earth with a bump.

'You couldn't hurt him. He's barely human. Anyway, he hasn't cared about your feelings, has he? The two of you have been more like brother and sister.'

'That's true,' she admitted ruefully.

'And you've craved for something more, haven't you?'

'I'd be less than human if I hadn't.'

He drew up before the flat and leaned back in his seat. 'Well, don't worry about it. Roger will find someone to partner him. His only passion seems tied up with sport. I don't know how you've managed to endure him so long.'

Wendy did not reply. Her mind was filled with speculation and wonder. Alan leaned towards her, kissing her lightly upon the lips, and she reached for his shoulders, then stopped herself almost shyly, aware that they were still little more than strangers. He put his arms around her and again she sank into a pool of ecstasy, almost unable to contain the emotions that became so vibrant and demanding in her mind.

'Now I think you'd better go in,' Alan murmured. 'You've had enough excitement for one evening, but tell me we'll do this again, Wendy.'

'Of course,' she replied without hesitation.

'All right, I'll say good night then.'

He walked around the car to help her out, then kissed her once again on the doorstep of the flat. Then he departed and Wendy watched him drive away, her mind filled with a complexity of emotions and thoughts. When she entered the flat she felt as if she were walking on air, and remained exhilarated as she undressed and went to bed. Sleep did not come easily, but when it did she slept badly, tossing and turning, keyed up by her experiences . . .

Next morning, when Wendy awoke to the shrill ringing of the alarm clock, she sat for a moment gazing at the sunlight peering in at the window, her thoughts meandering over the previous evening.

'Come on, sleepy-head!' Anne's voice sounded through the door, and she pounded upon the panels. 'We'll be late if you don't hurry.'

Wendy smiled and arose, then went to the bathroom to prepare for the day's duty. Her head seemed to be still in the clouds and when she went into the little kitchen for breakfast she found it difficult to concentrate upon Anne's questions.

'My word,' commented her friend, 'Alan certainly had a strange effect upon you! I'm afraid you'll have to pull yourself together for duty or you'll never get through the day.' Anne pointed at the toast that was getting cold. 'Hurry it up or we'll be in trouble.'

Wendy ate her breakfast and they departed for the hospital. When they entered the reception area and parted, she found Roger waiting in the corridor for her. He came towards her with a faint grin.

'Hello,' he said, falling into step beside her. 'I'm not seeing so much of you these days. I'm off duty this evening. Can we get together for a game of tennis?'

'I don't know!' Wendy remembered all that Alan had said about Roger and his passion for tennis. 'To tell you the truth I'm going off the game a little.'

'Impossible.' He shook his head slowly. 'I'll never believe that. But you didn't play last night, did you? I heard that you weren't at the centre.'

'No. Alan wanted to go out for the evening, so we dined out. It made a complete change. We never seemed to get around to doing things like that.'

'I was always under the impression that you preferred to spend your free time playing tennis,' he countered. 'You introduced me to the game in the first place, if you remember.'

'I remember, but you were also very keen.' Wendy turned to face him, and his eyes seemed filled with uneasiness.

'You're changing,' he observed softly. 'I've seen it coming, and I think Alan's arrival has finally unbalanced you.'

'I don't know what you mean by that. I only went out with Alan in the first place because you asked me to. But I will be truthful with you, Roger. I have become rather impatient with the way my life has been moving along.'

Roger glanced ahead. They were rapidly approaching Women's Surgical. 'Look, we can't talk here, Wendy. May I see you this evening? I don't think we'd better go to the sports centre. Perhaps there are other things we should talk of.'

'Certainly. I'd like nothing better.'

'All right. I'll call for you around seven-thirty. Will that be all right?'

'Fine. I'll be looking for you.'

Wendy frowned as she entered the ward and halted her flow of personal thoughts. It was all too easy to slip into her routine, and Sister Gilbert appeared but did not issue any orders. Wendy was pleased about that. It proved she was showing that she could work without supervision, and that was the next step to taking charge herself.

But there were setbacks that morning, and a mix-up with two patients that could have proved calamitous but for Wendy's alertness. Sister Gilbert lost her calm manner for the first time in many years, and blamed herself for the incident which almost resulted in Mrs. Parkes having a hysterectomy instead of a repair and Mrs. Wenn having a repair instead of a full hysterectomy. When the matter had been sorted out and a junior nurse dismissed from the ward, Sister Gilbert thanked Wendy for the part she had played.

'There'll be a stink over this,' she said. 'I'm responsible and I'll get a rocket for it, but you acted with commendable vigilance, Nurse, and that will go into my report. We all make mistakes, I know, but a nurse isn't permitted to make a human error when on duty.'

'I agree,' Wendy observed, 'but you

were not really to blame for what happened, Sister.'

'I'm responsible for the ward and the blame must fall upon my shoulders. The lesson is there for you to learn. I can't stress too firmly the need for checking and rechecking. Did you think I was too harsh on that junior?'

'No. It will teach her to be careful in future and the lesson may save a patient's life.'

'Quite right. I'll have a quiet talk with her later, to take the sting out of my words. The poor kid was crying as she left the ward and she is most promising.' Sister Gilbert turned away. 'No doubt I'll catch it from Mr. Holbrook when he gets to hear about it, but my back is broad. Take over here now, Nurse. I'll be back in fifteen minutes.'

Wendy's expression was serious as she watched Sister Gilbert's departure. The incident had shaken them all and Wendy made a mental note to be on her guard against permitting personal feelings to intrude upon duty. As Sister Gilbert disappeared along the passage the stocky figure of Alan Scott appeared and Wendy tightened her lips as she watched his approach.

She didn't want to talk to him now and could feel no emotion at all in her mind. He came to her, self-assured and aware of his power over her. She knew that he had their personal situation completely under control, but she was on duty and steeled herself.

'You don't have a patient in this ward, do you, Doctor?' she asked sternly.

'No, I don't,' he replied, frowning. 'I've come to have a quick word with you.'

'I wish you wouldn't.' Her voice did not waver. 'We almost had a tragic mistake in here a short time ago because a nurse let her concentration slip. Sister Gilbert will be in trouble because of it. I don't want you to talk about personal issues when I'm on duty.'

'There's more to it than that, isn't there?' he retorted. 'I've heard that you and Roger are going out for the evening — and not to the sports centre.'

'That's right. Or we may not go out at all. Roger is coming round to the flat, but that has nothing to do with duty and I'm afraid that I must get on. Please excuse me.'

She was aware that her tone was harsh and impersonal, but she was still shocked by what had happened. He nodded slowly and turned away. As he departed she wondered about the previous evening, but could not decide just how important to her he was. And what about Roger? Where did he fit into her life? She suddenly realized that she had no idea of what she wanted, and that fact alone proved just how aimless her personal life was. Nothing had really changed, except that she was now involved with two men instead of one, and that made for complications which she could well do without.

3

Promptly at seven-thirty that evening the doorbell rang and Anne started up, dropping the magazine through which she had been idly flicking, but Wendy arose, motioning with her hand.

'That will be Roger, I expect,' she remarked. 'I'll get it.'

'I'm expecting Derek at any time,' said Anne. 'I'd better get a move on.'

As Wendy opened the door, expecting to see Roger, she found Anne's friend, Derek, standing there.

'Hello,' he said. 'Playing tennis this evening?'

'No. Won't you come in? Anne is almost ready.'

'Thanks.' He crossed the threshold and walked toward the sitting-room. 'That will be the day when she's ready on time. I think she does it deliberately, you know.'

'That's one of the burdens a man has to shoulder, isn't it?' Wendy remarked.

Then the doorbell rang again. 'Excuse me. That will be Roger.'

'Your boy-friend?'

'A doctor at the hospital. We have been friends for years.'

Wendy went to answer the door. She drew a long breath as she opened it, and looked into Roger's impassive face.

'Hello,' he said. 'I'm a few minutes late. I was held up at the hospital.'

'That's all right. Come on in.' She waited until he was in the hall, then closed the door. 'Go into the sitting-room. Anne's friend is there. They're going out as soon as she is ready.'

He nodded and walked ahead of her. As she introduced him to Derek and watched him greet the man, she watched him critically, but there was no definite feeling in her mind for him. He occupied a great deal of her life because they had been friends for years, but she sensed that if he suddenly dropped out of her daily round she would not miss him too much.

'I don't know how you can do your job,' Derek commented, shaking his head. 'I'm terrified by the thought of having to go into hospital. I've been fortunate, so far, in that I haven't been seriously ill, but I don't know how I'd fare if it ever came to the worst.'

'A lot of people feel like that,' said Roger, seating himself by the window and folding his arms, 'but they adapt to the situation and quickly realize that we are there just to help them.'

'Your work is worth while of course.' Derek nodded. 'Now I don't have much justification for living. I sell cars. That's no great help to the community.'

'The majority of families have cars,' observed Wendy, 'and someone has to sell them.'

'Perhaps you're right.' Derek smiled. He arose, for Anne appeared in the doorway at that moment. 'All ready?' he demanded. 'The age of miracles is not past!'

'I've been waiting for you,' Anne retorted. 'I've been ready for some time. Hello, Roger, how are you?'

'Hello.' Roger got to his feet. 'You're looking well, Anne.'

'It's all the exercise we get trotting around the wards,' Anne replied with a grin. She glanced at Wendy. 'We're off now. I don't think I shall be very late, but be sure and set your alarm clock, just in case.'

'All right,' Wendy murmured. 'Have a nice time.'

'I'll probably see you again,' said Derek, glancing at Roger.

'You're sure to if you come around here very often,' Roger countered.

Wendy wondered about that remark as Anne and Derek departed, and when they were alone she looked into Roger's face. He was watching her and she wondered what was on his mind.

'This makes a change,' she said brightly. 'Can I get you a drink, Roger?'

'No, thank you. Come and sit down. I want to talk to you.'

She moved to the settee and sat down, where he joined her, stretching out his long legs. 'I've been giving a great deal of thought to us,' he went on. 'We've known each other for a number of years and we've been the best of friends.'

'That's stating the obvious,' Wendy muttered.

'I know. I'm just trying to get round to what I want to say. I don't know why I should find myself tongue-tied, but I suppose I've been too content to live as we have been doing. Days come and go with little change in routine and one tends to take some things for granted. Anyway, I have seen a change in you recently, and I've gained some impressions on what it's about, but I'd like to hear your views. Just what is on your mind?'

'How do I answer that?'

'Truthfully?' he suggested.

'I'd certainly be truthful.' She shrugged. 'Really, there isn't anything to consider. I've got to the stage where I feel that we've got into a rut. You were quite happy to go along with it, but something inside me demanded a change.'

'That's natural enough. What did you have in mind?'

'That's a bit cold-blooded, isn't it?'

'Perhaps that is the whole problem. Perhaps you find me too cold-blooded, Wendy.'

'I find your impersonal attitude towards me rather perplexing, shall we say?'

'My impersonal attitude?' he echoed. 'By that I suppose you mean my respect for you. I didn't think you wanted me to treat you as most men treat women these days. I'm talking of the permissive society.'

'I don't go for that kind of thing myself, but you've got to admit that we've been friends for a long while, and it just isn't natural for a friendship like ours to remain so static.'

He smiled thinly. 'Don't you remember the conversation we had when we first started going around together?'

'Refresh my memory.'

'I told you my burning ambition is to have my own nursing home and I've been working towards that end for a long time. I said that I didn't want to become involved with any woman because she would divert me from my original plan.'

'But it is inhuman for a man to cut himself off from normal human contact because of a dream.'

'It isn't a dream. It's fast becoming a reality. I have a great-aunt who is leaving me a great deal of money when she dies — and she's eighty-seven now. I hope that doesn't sound too material-istic, but that is the situation and I need a clear mind to handle this business. When I'm settled in the nursing home and have it running properly I'll then be able to give some thought to myself. I've told you all this before, Wendy.'

Wendy paused for a moment, decided that, yes, she had heard all this before and went on brusquely: 'Look, you asked to see me this evening and I fancy it was because Alan took me out to dinner last night. If you are so set on your ambitions and have no regard for me then go ahead and work it all out, but don't try to monopolize me any longer. I have no ambitions beyond becoming a Sister and doing my duty, but I am also human and I need some contact with others.'

'I'm in love with you, Wendy,' he said softly, and the words struck her dumb in amazement. 'I've never said anything to you because there didn't seem to be any hurry. You seemed happy enough with the way our lives were running together and I didn't want any complications before I settled my ambitions, but you're on the wrong track if you think I don't care about you.'

'Why didn't you demonstrate your feelings?' she demanded. 'If you had only given me a hint that would have been sufficient, but you made me feel that all I was fit for was a tennis partner. It wasn't enough and I've been getting moody about it.'

'Which is a natural reaction.' He nodded. 'I may seem to be a cold fish to you, but I've got my priorities right. This is the only way to handle my life.'

'And what am I supposed to do?' She studied his face, indecisive because of his admission of love, but there were no bells ringing in her mind and she knew only a sense of emptiness when she ought to have been singing in joy.

'I could ask you to wait for me, but that hardly seems fair under the circumstances. It didn't seem to matter while you were uninterested in anyone else, but now Alan is interested in you I fear that the situation will slip from my grasp.'

'How long would I have to wait?'

He sighed and shook his head. 'I don't know. It depends upon my aunt.'

'You mean I would have to wait until she died before you could even consider a future which might include me?'

'I don't seem to have much option, do I? I wouldn't want to raise your hopes, only to have to dash them later.

That's why I haven't permitted a normal relationship to develop between us. I'm trying to be fair to you.'

'You don't even act human,' she retorted. 'I don't know what to make of you, Roger.'

'You could try telling me what your attitude is towards me.'

'That's just it. I don't know! We've been tennis partners for four years and that's the sum total of our friendship. How do you expect me to feel about you? I've never heard an endearment pass your lips.'

'You could be to blame for that.' He smiled ruefully. 'You're so unapproachable! You're not the kind of girl a man could flirt with.'

'Thank you!' Her eyes sparkled with anger.

'I mean that as a compliment, and you know I'm not the type to flirt.' He shrugged. 'I think I'm just getting into deep water trying to make an explanation. If you can't put two and two together and come up with an answer you want then I suggest that we don't see each other for a spell.'

'You tell me that you love me, but you say it as if you're telling a patient she has pneumonia or something. You don't even show affection, Roger.'

'You know I'd give my right arm to have Alan Scott's manner. He's made more progress with you in a week than I have in four years.'

'Am I that difficult to get along with?' she demanded.

'No.' He sighed heavily. 'It isn't you, it's me. I don't know where I've gone wrong, but when we didn't become more than friends it became all the more difficult to do something about it.'

When Wendy thought of all the times they had been out together she knew she could not turn her back completely upon their friendship — but could romance follow now? She doubted it. She didn't feel romantically inclined towards him. Alan Scott's kisses the evening before had awakened some-thing intangible inside her. There was no way back to the degree of friendship which had existed for her and Roger. They could only go on to other things or finish.

'What do you want me to do, Wendy?' Roger asked quietly. 'Shall I stop seeing you? Is that what you want?'

'You say that you love me. Are you prepared to let me go now, if I ask?'

'If you want to leave me then I'd agree to it for your sake, but I certainly don't want that to happen.'

'Then what do you want?'

'I don't think I really count in this. It's what you want that matters.'

'All right, so let's forget about it for a time, shall we? You go your way and I'll go mine. I wouldn't have an easy conscience if I thought that I might be preventing you from realizing your ambitions.'

He stood up and she arose, too, and walked to the window. The sun was still shining on the garden, but it was low in the sky and shadows were long across the grass. Roger came to stand behind her and she could hear his breathing. Then he placed his hands upon her shoulders, gripping hard.

'Wendy, I think more than enough has been said. You have found Alan interesting and nothing I say is going to stop you from seeing him. I am in love with you, but I feel that I have something else to accomplish in life. I'm thirty-two this year and if I don't begin to make a decisive move it will be too late.'

'I've heard you talk on more than one occasion about the nursing home, but I didn't know it was all you dreamed about.' She made no attempt to turn and face him. 'It's the kind of rival I cannot compete against, I'm afraid. I think perhaps we ought to follow your suggestion and not see each other.'

'All right.' He took his hands from her shoulders. 'I'll leave now. See you at the hospital. Don't bother to see me out — I know the way.'

Wendy fought the impulse to stop

him, but she heard the door open, then close, and clenched her hands as she gazed unseeingly across the garden. It was over between them.

The sound of his car departing broke the paralysis which seemed to grip her and she turned from the window, pacing the room while she tried to come to grips with the new situation.

A sense of loneliness assailed her but she fought it off. She would certainly miss Roger because her whole off-duty life had been centred around him, but she had begun to chafe at that particular existence so this development was exactly right for her.

The evening dragged on, the silence of the house bearing down upon her. She tried to read, but found it impossible to concentrate. When it was time to go to bed she was relieved and, although she slept badly, was happier next morning when she had to report for duty.

It was Anne's day off, so Wendy walked alone to the hospital. When she reported to Sister Gilbert she discovered that some changes had taken place on the ward because of the events of the previous day. Sister Gilbert called her into the little office and closed the door. Her usually serene expression was gone and her eyes showed signs of anger.

'There was quite a to-do after you went off duty,' reported her superior. 'Mr. Holbrook almost brought down the hospital. If it had been Mr. Butler he would have played it down by saying that the mistake didn't take place and no harm was done. I've got to go on the carpet for it, anyway, and you're to take a more active part in running this ward. I'm to report upon the way you handle it and then you'll get your promotion. I'm happy for you, and if you do take over Women's Surgical I'll go on to something else.'

'They're not pushing you out because of what happened yesterday, are they?'

'No. I'm expecting promotion, and I

can thank you that there isn't a black mark against me. I shudder to think of what might have happened yesterday, but that is all so much water under the bridge, thank heavens! Let's get to work. You carry on as if you were the Sister in charge and I'll merely remain in the background, watching points. I have taken over from the night nurse, but you know all about checking reports, don't you?'

'Yes, Sister.' Wendy nodded and felt a weight slip from her mind as she prepared to throw herself into duty. It was a relief to be able to forget about personal issues and she made a vow as she entered the ward never to let her own life intrude upon work.

The morning went smoothly and Sister Gilbert complimented Wendy on the way she handled the ward. Three cases for surgery went down to the Theatre and returned without incident. Then there was an emergency case brought in, a woman in her forties who was pregnant but showing signs of miscarriage, and Mr. Holbrook arrived to examine the patient. Wendy had to be present, while Sister Gilbert remained in the background, and Mr. Holbrook, a tall, solid man in his late forties, eyed Wendy keenly. He had greying hair and sandy-coloured eyes, and his manner was brusque, his voice loud and penetrating.

'Nurse Curtis,' he said as they entered into the screened-off bed area of the new admission. 'Thank goodness there was someone in the ward yesterday who knew what was going on. I'm glad we'll be working together in future. I'm sure we'll get along.'

'Thank you, Mr. Holbrook,' Wendy replied, and remained at the foot of the bed while he examined the patient.

Mr. Holbrook asked questions which the woman, Mrs. Sanderson, answered in nervous tones. Then he glanced at Wendy. 'Have her ready in the Theatre in an hour, would you please, Nurse?'

'Yes, Mr. Holbrook.' Wendy pulled back the screens as he departed.

Sister Gilbert approached and Wendy reported what had taken place.

'Good. You're doing all right, Nurse. Carry on. I know that Mr. Holbrook wants to work with you, but it's if you get on the wrong side of him that you have to watch out.'

'He's one of the best though, isn't he?'

'He certainly is — and he knows it. That's the trouble. He expects everyone to have the same dedication and degree of efficiency. I agree that he should expect and get nothing less than the highest standards, but he doesn't make life easy for us.'

Wendy left the ward then, taking her break, and, as she was returning afterwards, met Alan Scott in the corridor.

'Hello,' he said, 'I've been hanging around in the hope of bumping into you. What about this evening? Doing anything in particular?'

Wendy was about to say that she would have to check with Roger when she recalled that the old way of life was over.

'No,' she replied. 'I'm doing nothing at all.'

'I heard from Roger what happened last night,' he continued. 'I must say that you don't seem very upset.'

'I told you that Roger was nothing more than a friend and as we are going our separate ways there's no reason why either of us should be upset.' She studied Alan's face, wondering why she felt so unemotional now. A few days ago she had been wanting romance, but now her feelings seemed blunted and despite the fact that romance was hers for the taking she felt strangely remote about the whole business.

'You don't want to play tennis, do you?' he asked.

'Not really. I'm working even harder in the ward now. Sister Gilbert is putting me through my paces. I think I'm expected to take over from her shortly.'

'That's the word going the rounds

and I also heard about yesterday's business. You were quite right to rebuke me for coming into the ward to talk of personal matters.'

He sounded contrite and there was a sorrowful expression on his face which he greatly exaggerated. When she smiled he nodded.

'That's better. You keep smiling. What would you like to do this evening? Shall I call for you?'

'Yes, if you wish, but I don't fancy going out for a formal evening.'

'All right. Perhaps we can sit in and talk. Will your flat-mate be there?'

'I doubt it. She doesn't stay in if she can help it.'

'I don't blame her. Life is too short for any of it to be wasted.'

'And you think I've been wasting my life for four years, don't you?' Wendy asked.

'That's my opinion, but, of course, you may hold an entirely different view. Anyway, I must go now. See you at your flat at about seven.'

'Yes. I'll be looking for you.'

Then he departed, and she watched him, noting the jaunty angle of his head, the way he swung his arms, and she knew that life would never be dull with him . . .

Wendy went off duty with Sister Gilbert's praises ringing in her ears and met Roger in the car park as she made her way to the exit.

'Hello,' he said gently. 'How are you this morning?'

'Fine, thank you.' She did not pick him up on the fact that the morning was past and it was almost the middle of the afternoon.

'Seeing Alan this evening?'

'Yes.'

'But you won't be going to the sports centre, I should imagine.' His voice was steady, almost impersonal. 'I have the feeling that you'll give up tennis altogether now.'

'What about you?' she countered. 'Are you still going down there?'

'Of course. There's a new nurse,

Marjorie Blake, who can play a bit.'

'I hope you'll get along with her.'

'I'm sure to.' He chuckled dryly. 'I get along with everyone. Well, I'd better be on my way. See you around, Wendy.'

'Good-bye,' she answered, and turned away. She felt cold inside as she walked through the park on her way home. It wasn't easy to forget a man who had played such a prominent part in her life for four years — but he had already forgotten about her, it seemed . . .

That evening when Alan arrived, Wendy was still in a hyper-critical mood. She watched him intently as they sat and talked and she found herself comparing him with Roger, which was not fair to either man. Then Derek arrived and Alan greeted him with an easy, familiar manner. They chatted until Anne was ready and then they both left. Almost before the front door had closed behind them Alan was taking Wendy into his arms and she found herself in a quandary, for despite the fact that she had craved his kisses and embraces only a few days before, this evening she found the experience stifling.

'What's wrong?' Alan released her and sat back, eyeing her closely. 'You're not in the mood for me, are you? Would you rather go out for a drink instead?'

'No, thank you.'

'Well, do you play chess? Or how about cards? I want to prove to you that I am a home-loving man. I'm prepared to do anything to show you that I care.'

'You care about me?' Wendy murmured. 'You haven't known me two weeks.'

'Time doesn't enter into it. The minute I set eyes upon you I knew you were the girl for me.'

'How many girls have you said that to?'

'Don't be fooled by my carefree attitude. I'm very serious underneath.'

He took her into his arms again and kissed her gently. Wendy found pleasure in it, but the urgency was gone from her mind and Alan sensed it. He shook his head ruefully as he released her.

'This isn't my night,' he observed. 'But I can wait. I'm a patient man.'

'You're full of virtues,' Wendy pointed out. 'I have a reputation for being patient myself.'

'So I've heard.' He smiled. 'You must have the patience of Job, the way you waited around for Roger.'

'I'd feel happier if you didn't mention him,' she retorted. 'That's a part of my life that's over and done with and I don't want to be reminded of it.'

'Sorry, but I can hardly believe my luck in that quarter. I didn't think you'd give him up.'

'There was nothing to give up — except friendship.' She narrowed her eyes as she considered Roger and again sensed that all was not well in the back of her mind, but she could not put her finger upon the exact reason for feeling uneasy and suppressed a sigh as she tried to enter into Alan's light-hearted manner.

By the time he left her Wendy was feeling easier, telling herself that he was just the type she needed to help her forget about Roger.

★   ★   ★

Time did begin to heal the scar that parting from Roger had caused, although she would not admit to herself that she did miss him. But as the days went by and she saw more and more of Alan she felt easier in his company and began to look forward to his kisses and embraces. Her heart still seemed to lurch whenever she came into contact with Roger around the hospital, which, fortunately, was rarely, and she refused to go to the sports centre, although Alan asked her to several times. When she told him flatly that she did not want to play tennis again he came back at her with alacrity.

'I think you're afraid of meeting

Roger down there,' he accused. 'You two haven't seen each other off duty since I stepped into his shoes.'

'You didn't step into his shoes!' Wendy retorted angrily. 'If you believe that then you are mistaken. Roger never kissed me seriously in all the years we were together.'

'Then he was a bigger fool than I imagined.' Alan chuckled and put his arms around her, but Wendy fobbed him off.

'I don't like your attitude,' she said slowly. 'Since Roger dropped out of my life you've become very dominant.'

'I'm sorry, but no two men are alike. Roger was a doormat. He couldn't make a decision if he tried.'

'I don't like the way you denigrate him. He's one of the finest doctors at the hospital.'

'No one is disputing the fact. All I'm saying is that as a man his manner leaves a lot to be desired.'

Wendy took a deep breath. There were times when Alan aggravated her.

She studied him, taking in his manner, listening to his conversation, and she slowly realized that he was a stranger to her, a man she had quite a lot to learn about, and she fancied that her desire to find romance had compelled her to throw caution to the winds. He was not her type! Once she had come to that conclusion she began to experience a strange desire for the old, comfortable evenings she used to spend with Roger . . .

It was Wendy's week-end off duty and she planned to go home to see her parents, but when she mentioned it to Alan he suggested accompanying her.

'I can get the week-end off. I'm sure Roger will change duties with me. I'd like to meet your parents. What does your father do for a living?'

'He's a farmer. He lives in the Manor House at Broughton.'

'A gentleman farmer, by the sound of it. What about it, Wendy? Shall I try to get the time off?'

'If you wish.' She felt a strange reluctance gripping her as she spoke. Roger had been home with her many times and her parents liked him. She had not informed them of the great change in her life and wondered what they would have to say if she turned up with a different man.

'I'll talk to Roger, then.' Alan glanced at his watch. 'I suppose I'd better be going now. I've got to be at the hospital early in the morning. I'll see you tomorrow.'

She saw him to the door and he kissed her before departing. Wendy returned to the sitting-room to ponder over the situation. It was daunting to realize that she could not find complete happiness in Alan's company. There were a number of small things about him which disturbed her, although she could not really pinpoint them, and she felt a growing conviction that she did not want to take him home.

Acting upon impulse, Wendy telephoned Roger's flat, and when he answered she felt awkward and tongue-tied.

'It's Wendy,' she said.

'Hello. This is a surprise. Nothing wrong, is there?'

'No, nothing wrong,' she replied. 'I just wanted to ask a favour of you. I don't really know how to put it, but Alan is going to ask you to change duties with him this week-end. I'm going home and he wants to come with me.'

'That's all right. When I see him I'll tell him that I'll swop with him.'

'No, you don't understand! I don't want to take him home with me, but I also don't want to raise any complications by telling him that in so many words. Would you tell him that you've already made other arrangements?'

'I understand. You know, one of the things I'm going to miss is going with you. I love Broughton. Your parents have always made me welcome.'

'Yes, they like you. Well, thank you,

Roger, and I'm obliged for the favour.'

'Think nothing of it.' He chuckled. 'See you around, Wendy.'

★　★　★

Next morning, just after Doctor's Round, Alan entered Women's Surgical and held up a hand as he faced Wendy.

'I know I shouldn't be here,' he said quickly as she glanced around to locate Sister Gilbert, 'but I just had to let you know that I won't be able to make it this week-end.'

'Oh, I'm sorry!' Wendy frowned as she spoke, for she hated to lie. 'But there will be other times, Alan.'

'The trouble is, I'm not on duty all week-end, but the off-duty periods are definitely anti-social.' He paused. 'Do you have to go home?'

'Yes. I'm sorry, but I can't cancel the trip now.'

'How do you get there?'

'By bus.'

'When do you leave?'

'Friday afternoon — as soon as I get off duty.'

'I'm off Friday evening, but I'll have to be back by ten. I could drive you home if you waited until five-thirty.'

'No, I couldn't let you do that. By the time we arrived you'd have to turn around and come back. It wouldn't be fair. I'll catch a bus and make my usual trip.'

'Roger has been to your place a number of times, hasn't he?'

'Yes.'

'Have you told your parents that you've finished seeing him?'

'No.'

'Then it's just as well that I'm not going down with you, eh? It might give them a shock to have you turn up with a total stranger, although I'm not a stranger to you any more, am I?'

'You certainly aren't!' Wendy smiled. 'Now I must get on, Alan.'

He nodded. 'I'll call for you this evening around seven,' he said, turning away. 'See you then.'

'All right. I'll be ready.' Wendy returned to her work and found a niggling sensation in her mind. She had detested her subterfuge and felt extremely guilty about it. But, more than that, she was concerned that she had not desired his company over the week-end. Her disinclination had to prove something, but exactly what she could not tell.

It seemed that Roger still had some power over her and she tried to analyse her feelings as she went about her duties — but the harder she tried to get a clear answer the more muddled she became.

4

It was a relief for Wendy to get away on Friday afternoon and she sighed heavily as she left the hospital and walked through the park on her way home. Anne was already there and she chatted while Wendy packed her bag.

'How are you getting along with Alan?' she asked, standing in the doorway of Wendy's bedroom.

'There's nothing serious,' Wendy said without hesitation.

'So he's not Mr. Right!'

'I find him nice enough, but I have a feeling there could never be anything between us.'

'That's all right then.' Anne seemed relieved and Wendy went back to her packing. 'What about Roger? Have you seen him lately?'

'Only about the hospital.'

'Well, he's getting very thick with

Marj Blake. They're playing tennis almost every evening they're free.'

'I'd be greatly surprised if they didn't!' Wendy said wryly. 'That's all Roger's life consists of.'

'There's got to be more to him than duty and tennis. Did you ever find out what really makes him tick?'

'Yes.' Wendy nodded as she closed her small case. 'That's why we finally parted. There's no room in his life for romance. I felt that our friendship had gone as far as it could and there was no point in going on.' She glanced at her watch. 'Time I was going or I'll miss my bus. See you on Sunday, Anne.'

Her friend walked to the door with her. 'I'll keep an eye on things around here,' she promised. 'Go and forget all about Halesborough and everything in it. Have a nice time and come back with a fresh outlook on life.'

'Do I look as if I need it?' Wendy answered, smiling. She departed and, as she walked to the bus station, she wondered exactly what she did want. She seemed uncertain deep within her, and hoped a complete change of scenery would help clarify the situation.

★   ★   ★

The spring evening, when Wendy reached Broughton and telephoned the Manor House for her father to come and pick her up, was warm and bright and she sat on the wooden seat by the war memorial waiting for the first glimpse of her father's Rover.

Her thoughts were nostalgic. The last time she had come home Roger had been with her. She looked around critically. The little market town was quiet. The church clock chimed seven-thirty and then a car pipped its horn and she looked up to see her father smiling at her. Wendy took up her bag, hurrying towards the car, and William Curtis leaned across and opened the door for her.

'Hello, Wendy,' he said, taking her

face in his hands and kissing her. 'You were day-dreaming when I arrived. Don't tell me you miss this old town.'

'Hello, Father.' She hugged him. 'It's nice to see you. How's Mother?'

'Fine. She's keeping well — but you haven't brought Roger along!'

'No.' Wendy paused for the merest second. 'He couldn't get away.'

'I see. So you'll have a quiet week-end with us, eh?' He slipped into gear and pulled away from the kerb.

'The place doesn't change at all,' Wendy observed as her father drove over a bridge spanning a narrow river.

'Places like these don't change much over the years — it's only the people who change.'

'But some people don't change.'

'You sound as if you've suffered a little since we last saw you. Is anything wrong?'

'No.' Wendy shook her head. 'There's nothing wrong, Father. I'm tired, that's all.'

She sat up a little straighter as her

father slowed the car, then turned into a driveway and followed it towards a large, red-brick manor house that was surrounded by poplars and oaks. The tyres crunched on the gravel and the car halted smoothly before the grey steps leading up to the front door.

'There's your mother now,' said her father as she opened the car door. 'She's been impatient to see you.'

Wendy hurried up the steps and kissed her mother's cheek.

Mrs. Curtis was tall and slender, a very young fifty-six. 'I'm so glad you've come home,' she said. 'We don't see enough of you — but Roger isn't with you! Couldn't he get away?'

'Roger and I haven't been seeing so much of each other lately.' Wendy spoke casually, aware that she needed to drop a hint in order to pave the way for an announcement later in her changed circumstances.

Mrs. Curtis glanced at her, arching her eyebrows, and Wendy forced a smile.

'You don't seem too surprised, Mother,' she remarked.

'I've always sensed that Roger wasn't the marrying kind.'

'What's marriage got to do with it?'

'When two people go around together as long as you and Roger have, then marriage begins to rear its head. If one of you has no intention of marrying then the other drifts away.'

'You make it sound simple, but that's exactly what did happen though, so I'd better tell you now.' She heard her father's approach but continued in even tones, trying to sound more casual than she actually felt. When she had explained what had happened she saw her mother nod briefly.

'I have been expecting this, Wendy,' said Mrs. Curtis. 'I'm not surprised.'

'But it isn't that Roger doesn't care about me,' added Wendy, and went on to explain about Roger's ambitions.

'That's no excuse,' cut in her father. 'A man in love with a woman wouldn't let anything put him off. I've always liked Roger, as you know, but the way he's been keeping you on a string makes me suspect his motives.'

'Well, we've parted for the time being.' Wendy hoped she sounded carefree, but there was a certain tension in her voice which could give her away. 'Anyway, I'm seeing a lot of another doctor who has just come to the hospital.' She paused for a moment and then changed the subject. 'You'll be pleased to hear that my promotion to Sister is on the cards at last. I'm being trained in Women's Surgical now and Sister Gilbert thinks I'll be taking over very shortly.'

'That's what you've always wanted, isn't it?' asked her mother.

'Of course. That's the height of my ambition.'

'You mean you can't go higher?'

'I could, but not yet, I'll need more qualifications before I can set my sights even higher. But I like working with the patients. I feel that I'm doing a worthwhile job if I can actually see people getting better as a result of what I do.'

'You're dedicated,' her father said with a chuckle. 'And to think that I offered you a job as a secretary! But you did look a bit broody when I first saw you in town. I had the feeling that you were just picking yourself up off the floor.'

'Things tend to get on top of me,' remarked Wendy. 'But enough of my way of life. Let me take my things up to my room, then we can sit down and have a good natter. I've got a lot of catching up to do with local affairs.'

* * *

Saturday seemed such a long day to Wendy. She went shopping with her mother during the morning, then, after lunch, changed into jeans and stout shoes and went for a walk around the farm.

She pondered deeply as she walked, taking in the familiar sights, and came to several conclusions before the afternoon was over. She would stop seeing Alan. There was nothing for him in her heart. She had thought that he would slowly take over her feelings when Roger departed, but that had not been the case. She knew instinctively that Alan could never become dear to her, and looked upon him in much the same way that Roger had looked upon her — as a friend.

But Roger had professed love for her. She tingled at the thought. How could he love her and yet step aside for her to go out with another man? If his love was real then why would he risk losing her, and let the balance between his love and ambition swing against her?

She asked herself questions to which she could find no satisfactory answers and returned to the house resolved to make further changes in her life. When she entered the hall her mother appeared from the drawing-room.

'Wendy, there's been a call for you from the hospital. There's been some kind of an emergency there. One of the Sisters has been taken ill and you're wanted to go in and fill her place.'

'I see!' Wendy frowned as she turned to the telephone. 'I'd better call in and see what's going on.'

Wendy contacted the hospital and learned from the switchboard operator that the duty sister on Women's Surgical had reported sick and she was required to replace her.

'When am I needed?' Wendy asked.

'In the morning. Night Sister will be coming on earlier than usual, but you'll be required to take over the ward tomorrow morning.'

Wendy hung up and turned to face her mother. 'I'm sorry to be such a nuisance, but I ought to return this evening.'

'It's no bother. Father can drive you back. It will be an evening out for us. We hadn't made any other plans.'

'I'll go up and pack.' Wendy could feel anticipation welling up inside her as she turned to ascend the stairs. It struck her that everything should be working out fine now, and although she could not fault her professional life she had no idea how her personal life was going to develop . . .

After they had tea together, Wendy decided it was time to leave.

'I don't want you and Father getting back here too late,' she explained. 'If there was a bus I'd catch it, but the last one has gone.'

'You don't have to tell us about the local bus services,' her father replied. 'But don't worry, I feel like a drive this evening.'

Wendy sat in the back of the car with her mother while her father drove the fifty miles back to Halesborough. They chatted desultorily until they arrived. Wendy invited them up to the flat for coffee, but her father declined, saying that he had to be up early in the morning.

As it was still early, Wendy decided to go down to the sports centre, knowing that she wanted to see Roger rather than watch or play tennis. When she discovered that the tournament was nearing its final stages, and Roger and Marj Blake were still in the knockout competition, she felt her interest in the game perk up.

A number of her colleagues were present and she joined them, learning that Roger and Marj were favourites to win. When the pair came out to do battle she found that the sight of Roger filled her with trembling. All through their match she sat as if transfixed, scarcely taking her eyes off him, and her disappointment, when they lost, was hard to bear. Marj lost the game for them, she was aware, and knew that if she had been partnering Roger he would have won. She waited around despite the fact that some of her colleagues began to drift away and, shortly after, Roger and Marj appeared and she went to applaud their efforts.

'Hello, Wendy!' There was surprise in Roger's tones. 'What are you doing back here? I thought you'd gone for the entire week-end.'

She explained, then commiserated with them upon losing.

'It wasn't bad luck that we lost,' said Marj dejectedly. 'It was my playing. If you'd been partnering Roger he would have won, Wendy.'

'Nonsense!' exclaimed Roger. 'You did very well, Marj. You played better than I've seen you play before.'

'And it still wasn't good enough,' came the contrite reply. 'It's no good, Wendy. I can play with Roger in friendly matches, but when it comes to this competition stuff then he needs someone like you. If you'd been on the court instead of me he would have won.'

Marj smiled wearily and left them, and Wendy looked into Roger's face. His eyes were shining, as they always did after he'd played a particularly hard and fast game.

'Care for a coffee?' he offered.

'Thank you, I'd like one.' She stifled

a sigh as they fell into step and went towards the restaurant. It puzzled her, but the full circle her feelings had turned during the past few weeks was bringing her back to regard him as the only man she could really love. She wondered what it would be like to be kissed by him. Could he ever get emotional? She had never seen him aroused and could only guess at the way he would react.

When they were seated at a table, each with a coffee, he leaned back in his seat and regarded her steadily.

'How did you find Broughton?' he asked.

'It seemed a bit strange without you there,' she confessed. 'Mother and Father asked after you.'

'I wish I could have gone with you,' he replied, and her heart seemed to miss a beat at his words, 'but it's better that you go your way for a while in order to find out exactly what you want.'

'For a while?' she repeated. 'Does

that mean you'd like to get back on the old footing?'

'If you're agreeable to the terms I set,' he said slowly, 'but that wouldn't suit Alan.'

'What has Alan to do with it?'

'You have been seeing a great deal of him.'

'That doesn't mean a thing.'

'I noticed that he didn't bring you here at all.'

'He offered once or twice, but I didn't want to come.'

'So you're keen to come back to the old routine, are you?'

'Yes.' She nodded firmly.

'I was certain that you would, but you'll have to tell Alan.'

'I'll see him tomorrow. He'll be on duty.'

'What about Monday evening, then?' he queried. 'You'll be off duty. Shall we come here for a game?'

'I'd like to.' She smiled and he chuckled and drank his coffee. He seemed so sure of himself that she felt like washing her hands of the whole business, but the loneliness she had experienced was too depressing to be further endured. She told herself that she was extremely fortunate to be able to reverse the situation. Deep inside, she knew she was doing the right thing. He had stated that he was in love with her. She knew she was a patient type, so she would just have to assert her patience and wait for that moment when he could give her some personal attention, no matter how long it took.

★   ★   ★

Wendy awoke early on Sunday morning and contemplated the change in her fortunes. She was filled with elation and knew that it would be better to see Roger on a friendly basis than not to see him at all. Rising, she showered and prepared to go on duty, moving quietly around the flat so as not to awaken Anne. She then set out and walked to the hospital, arriving ten minutes before she was due to take up her duties.

The ward was quiet enough when she went into Women's Surgical and the night Staff Nurse was seated in the office.

'Hello,' she said, 'I heard they were bringing you in. There's nothing to report, although I've been warned that an emergency is coming in. Someone for observation — suspected appendix. Apart from that the ward is just as you left it on Friday.'

'Thanks. I'll go round and check the patients. You can get away now, if you're ready.'

'It looks like being a nice day. Pity I've got to sleep through the morning.' The Staff Nurse reached for her cape. She departed, pausing in the corridor to wait for her junior, and they went off together.

Wendy was greeted warmly by the patients and most of them expressed regret that she had been called in as a relief. Breakfast was over and there sounded the clatter of plates and dishes from the kitchen, where the orderlies were busy. Sunday would be quiet, Wendy told herself as she entered the office to go through the reports, apart from the visitors who would arrive later. Then a voice spoke from the doorway and she looked up to see one of the duty porters standing there.

'Nurse, we've got a Miss Devlone here — suspected appendix. Have you got a bed for her?'

'Yes. There's one ready on the left. Has she been examined?'

'Dr. Scott saw her. He'll be up in a moment,' he said. 'She's to be kept under observation.'

Wendy followed the porters into the ward. The new patient, a girl of about nineteen, looked rather pale and apprehensive and, when she had been put into bed, Wendy tried to reassure her.

'It's the first time I've been in hospital, Nurse,' came the reply.

'Don't worry. It's the first time for most patients. You're in good hands and you'll be perfectly all right. I'll need some details now, for the record.'

She made out a chart and took temperature and pulse-rate readings, and when she went back to the office Alan was there, waiting to talk to her.

'Hello,' he said. 'I was sorry they had to send for you.'

'It doesn't matter. I can always go home another time. Have you come to see the latest admission?'

'I've already seen her. We're to keep her under observation. You know what to do. No, I've come to talk to you, Sunday is a quiet day, so we needn't worry about you losing your concentration and making a mistake.'

Wendy smiled faintly. 'It won't be as quiet as you suggest when the visitors start coming in,' she retorted. 'But I'm glad you're here, Alan. I want to talk to you.'

'That sounds interesting. Tell me more.'

'I've been thinking about the situation that exists and I don't really like it. I'm going through a period of unrest and I'm going in any direction the wind happens to be blowing, so don't take this too much to heart, but I don't want to see you in future on a regular basis.'

'You what?' He was surprised and his eyes showed it. 'What's got into you now, Wendy?'

'Nothing. I told you, I'm in a state of flux at the moment. I don't know what I do want.'

'Say no more. I can tell by that expression on your face that I don't have a prayer of getting anywhere with you. It's written all over you — but I don't like it, Wendy. There'll be talk around the hospital.'

'Talk?' She frowned. 'What kind of talk?'

'About the way you're turning from one man to another.'

'Nonsense! I never listen to gossip and I've got no time for anyone who does.'

'All right, have it your way, but you'll fall back into your old habits and go straight back under Roger's thumb. In a couple of weeks you'll be as tied down as ever and you won't ever be able to get free of him again.' He turned away, pausing in the doorway of the office to glance at her. 'I'll be back later to check on that new patient.'

He left and Wendy went to the door to watch him walk along the corridor. A sense of relief spread through her. She had settled that particular matter and all she could do now was hope that by some miracle Roger would begin to accept her as a woman.

* * *

When Wendy went off duty that evening she was tired but relieved and was thankful that she had been recalled from home. Walking homeward in the gloom of the night, she stiffened her aching back and held her head up. Tomorrow she would play tennis with Roger and if he tried to remain impervious to her then she would attempt to sway him with womanly wiles. There was a great deal of truth in the saying that all was fair in love and war.

Anne was not home when she entered the flat, so Wendy made herself some coffee and sat down in the sitting-room to relax. Twenty minutes later, just as she was thinking of going to bed, the sound of the front door opening attracted her attention and Anne came in.

'Hello!' she called. 'I saw the light on and knew you were still up. Heard about you getting called back. But what's all this about you finishing with Alan and going back to Roger?'

'Where did you hear that?'

'Little birds have big beaks!' Anne chuckled. 'I was with Derek in the Goose and Lantern when Alan came in. He was in a bad mood, but Derek called him over and we heard the news from him. What's going on, Wendy? I've never known you to dither like this.'

'I'm not dithering,' Wendy retorted, frowning. 'Although I expect it looks like it. I'm merely trying to find myself. I don't know why I should be going through these moods, but my mind is beginning to clear.'

'So you're going back to Roger! That doesn't sound like progress to me.'

'It's quite simple.' Wendy got up. 'It's just a question of which man I'm happiest with.'

'And the answer to that is Roger, I assume!'

'That's the conclusion I've come to.' Wendy shrugged.

'But how can you be happy with a man who doesn't want to know about romance? You've fallen in love with him, but he's got other things on his mind. It wouldn't be so bad if it was golf or motor-racing he was hooked on. You could compete against those — but a nursing home! He seems to think he's got his priorities right, but he certainly hasn't. When it's too late he's going to realize that you're the only girl for him, and it would serve him right if you did find another man in the meantime.'

'I shan't even look for another,' said Wendy. 'Now I'm going to bed. I've had a tiring day.'

'I should think you have. You were out of the house a long time before I awoke and you've been on duty all day. What's it like running a ward on your own?'

'I wasn't on my own and it was very quiet, being Sunday. A lot more goes into it on a weekday, especially when there's an op's list to sort out.'

'Never mind. It's all good practice and you're destined for great things. Wendy, set your alarm for the morning, will you? I have a feeling that I'm going to find it difficult to wake up on time.'

Wendy nodded and they went to bed. For a long time Wendy lay considering the situation and realized that she was feeling a great deal happier. She slept peacefully, to awaken to the shrilling of the alarm clock, and she sprang out of bed and called to Anne as she dashed for the bathroom.

* * *

Going on duty, Wendy confronted Sister Gilbert in the office of Women's Surgical and her superior nodded knowingly as they exchanged greetings.

'So they sent for you, eh? That must prove something. I have orders to let you run the place today — you make the decisions and carry the can. I'll just be looking on as a spectator, or an umpire, if you like. I won't say a word unless I see something which looks like being a bad mistake cropping up, although I don't expect that to happen with you. Now let's get down to business, shall we? There are the reports, and the operations list. Mr. Holbrook is operating today, so you'll have to get the patients down to the Theatre on time or he'll be bellowing all over hospital. The first case is scheduled for nine-fifteen.'

Scanning the sheets and lists, Wendy then began her duties, ensuring that the nurses were working and that the patients due for operations were being prepared. She lost herself in the business and had the ward running smoothly.

Sister Gilbert was as true as her word. She remained in the background and not once did she have to intervene in Wendy's handling of the routine. A first-year nurse had been assigned to the ward and she seemed lost in the efficient working that went on around her. Wendy found the time to talk to her, trying to reassure her, remembering her own first days on a ward when everything seemed so difficult.

The morning passed so quickly that Wendy was surprised when Sister Gilbert approached her and offered to take over.

'Have I done something wrong, Sister?' demanded Wendy.

'Heavens, no! But if you look at the clock you'll see that it's time you went to have your break.'

'Is that the time?' Wendy stared at the clock in disbelief. 'Why, I imagined it was only about ten. Where's the time gone?'

'That's the way of it when you're running a ward,' came the wise reply. 'But you've been enjoying yourself this morning, haven't you? I can remember my days of training to take over. The world seemed to be a different place. Everything was a challenge. I almost envy you, knowing what's lying ahead of you, but we only have our time over once and perhaps that is as it should be. You'll do, Wendy. You've got the makings of a very fine Ward Sister — and don't let anyone tell you differently. I hope the world doesn't lose its shine for you. It's so easy to get into a rut and become disillusioned.'

'That will never happen to me while I can come into contact with patients,' Wendy declared, glancing around. The patients scheduled for operations that morning had all been down to the Theatre and there had been no complications. The appendix case who had been admitted the day before was still under observation and it seemed that an operation would not be necessary. 'I love this work and I hope I never have to leave it.'

'Well, you'd better leave it now and have your break,' said Sister Gilbert. 'I'll hold the fort until you come back.'

'Thank you, Sister.' Wendy went to the nurses' dining-room, but her thoughts were still occupied with all the events of the morning. Nurses were coming and going and then Anne appeared and sat opposite. She peered into Wendy's face for a moment before speaking, then reached out and shook Wendy's shoulder.

'Hey, it's me!' she said loudly. 'You're not getting proud these days, are you?'

'Oh, Anne!' Wendy pulled herself together. 'I didn't see you. I'm so busy trying to remember everything that's got to be done this afternoon. I've been running the ward today and I never knew a Sister had so much to think about. Heaven knows how everything gets done — it's a miracle there aren't more mistakes made.'

'Wendy, you're a real glutton for punishment. Now I would rather take orders than give them. All that responsibility would make me bow-legged.'

'I must get back to the ward,' Wendy murmured. 'See you later this evening. Are you going out?'

'That's a silly question. I'm on nights starting next week, so I'm going to make hay while the sun shines. Of course I'm going out. So are you, aren't you?'

'I arranged to play tennis with Roger.'

'Big deal!' Anne muttered. 'I'll have to get Derek to take me down there so I can see you play. I've heard a lot about your prowess. They're saying that you and Roger together would be unbeatable.'

'I don't know what Marj Blake will say when she knows I'm going to partner Roger again.' For a moment Wendy was concerned. 'I'll have to talk to her at the first opportunity. See you later, Anne.'

'Don't work too hard,' her friend retorted.

Wendy went back to the ward and immediately became engaged in its working. Mr. Holbrook and his registrar were in the office chatting with Sister Gilbert, and as soon as Wendy appeared Holbrook rounded upon her.

'Ah, there you are! Had a good lunch?'

'Yes, thank you, Mr. Holbrook,' she replied, trying to conceal her surprise.

'You did a fine job this morning, Nurse. I've been talking to Sister Gilbert about you. Those patients came down to Theatre right on the dot. That's what I like. Punctuality! If a nurse has that she has everything. I'm going to check out the patients I've operated on today. That appendix that you have in for observation. I'm not quite happy about her. As this is an operating day I think I'll have her down this afternoon. I don't want to get called out in the middle of the night.'

'What time would you like her in Theatre?' asked Wendy.

'I'll just take another look at her,' he said, eyeing her keenly. Then he smiled. 'Three o'clock will do. I'm going to have that appendix out.'

He departed then, followed by his registrar, and Sister Gilbert went with them, pausing in the doorway to glance back at Wendy.

'He's more than pleased with you. Keep up the good work. Another week like this and you'll be here without my backing.'

'I'll go over the reports, Sister,' Wendy replied, filled with pleasure by the praise.

When Wendy went off duty she was hardly able to think clearly. Her head was buzzing with all the events which had taken place and a small voice in her brain was repeating endlessly all the points she had needed to remember. As she reached the main entrance a voice hailed her and she saw Roger coming towards her.

'I've been waiting for you,' he said breathlessly. 'I can't get away yet. I'm standing in down at Casualty — there's been a pile-up on the motorway. We're waiting for the crash victims to be brought in. If you go down to the sports centre I'll meet you there as soon as I can. Now I must get moving. See you later.'

'One thing,' said Wendy as he began to move away. 'Have you managed to have a chat with Marj about me partnering you again?'

'I did exchange a few words with her this morning. There's nothing to worry about. She's not going down there this evening.'

'All right. I'll see you there.' Wendy went on her way as he darted off, only to be called again, this time by a female voice. She halted and turned to find herself confronted by Mrs. White, the Principal Nursing Officer.

'Nurse Curtis. If you're not in a

hurry I'd like a few words with you. The reports I've been getting about your progress are most gratifying and you'll be coming to see me in my office very soon now. The results of your last course indicate that you are above average to a high degree. Apart from that, Mr. Holbrook likes you, and I must have a Sister in charge of Women's Surgical who can get along with him. I'm relieved that we have found someone so suitable to replace Sister Gilbert.'

'Thank you, Mrs. White,' said Wendy, her pulses fluttering a little with excitement. 'I'm very happy to have the opportunity of working in Women's Surgical.'

'Keep up the good work. You're off duty now, aren't you? Go and enjoy yourself. You need to relax.'

Wendy was a little dazed by the way events were creeping up on her. It all seemed too good to be true! The thought crossed her mind and she mentally wished that Roger, too, would begin to see her in a different light — but she meant to work upon that problem as soon as she could and a smile flitted across her lips as she walked steadily homewards.

Anne was getting ready to go out when Wendy arrived and Derek was seated on the settee in the sitting-room. He grimaced as he greeted her.

'Still waiting for her!' he announced, glancing at his watch. 'Is she so unpunctual on duty? I can't believe that they'd let her get away with that in a hospital.'

'No. She's a very good nurse and I think she's deliberately taking it out on you because she has to be on her toes all day — but don't let on that I told you.' Wendy chuckled, but then he called to her.

'What are you doing this evening?'

'Playing tennis with Dr. Harley.'

'Aren't you too tired for that sort of thing after a shift on duty?'

'No. It's great fun.'

'Harley is the quiet one, isn't he?'

'That's right. Don't you like him?'

'Yes. He seems to be a decent type. It's the other one I don't like. You've given him up, haven't you?'

'Why the sudden interest?'

'I have a friend who wants to know you,' he replied. 'If you ever have a free evening then let me know and I'll fix a date.'

'I much prefer to arrange my own dates, thank you all the same!'

'I wish I'd met you before I met Anne,' Derek continued. 'I'd give those doctors a run for their money. I can't understand why one of them hasn't snapped you up.'

'Perhaps I don't want to be snapped up,' Wendy retorted.

'What's going on here?' demanded Anne, appearing from her bedroom. 'Not flirting with my man, are you, Wendy?'

'That would be the day,' Derek said, grinning. 'Wendy is duty-mad — and if it isn't duty then it's tennis.'

Wendy smiled wryly as she went

along to her room, for the description fitted Roger rather than herself — but pressure could be brought to bear upon him, and if it was judicially applied it might bring about the results she so desired. The important thing to remember, she told herself as she prepared to take a shower, was that she had nothing to lose and everything to gain. Roger thought he knew her, but he had a shock awaiting him — and the sooner she began her campaign the better.

5

When she arrived at the sports centre, Wendy went into the women's changing-rooms and prepared to play tennis, then went out to one of the courts and knocked a ball about with one of the nurses who had come down for a game. Time passed and she began to get anxious, for there was no sign of Roger. Then she saw his tall figure appearing from the men's changing-rooms and her heart seemed to miss a beat. She signalled Nurse Woolton to stop playing and they chatted until Roger arrived.

'You're playing a lot sharper than the last time,' said her colleague. 'Are you going to give Dr. Harley a beating?'

'I'm going to try to,' Wendy replied firmly. 'It might do him good.'

'Hello there,' greeted Roger, approaching quickly. 'Sorry I'm late, but we had a great deal to do. It was a nasty business. Anyway, let's not waste any more time, Wendy. Which end do you prefer?'

'It doesn't matter to me.' She smiled at Nurse Woolton, who moved away, and Roger jumped over the net and went to the far end.

They began to play and Wendy took it easy for the first few sets to get her eye in. She felt rusty, but soon found her form. Taking Roger by surprise, she won the set, and as they changed ends he paused to speak to her.

'You're taking it out on the ball, aren't you?' he inquired.

'No. I'm just pushing myself a bit to get back into the swing of things,' she said, and continued her attack during the next set.

Roger began to respond and soon they were battling it out as if they were playing in the final at Wimbledon. Wendy had always been as good a player as Roger, but with an edge on her determination she played that fraction of a degree better than usual.

She beat him decisively and he gazed at her with wonder in his eyes when they departed from the courts.

'You've never played like that before,' he accused. 'Are you trying to prove something?'

'No. Did it seem that I was? I was merely loosening up.'

'I wish you'd been with me in the tournament — we would have won it easily.'

'Never mind. Better luck next time.'

They changed and then went into the restaurant for coffee. Anne and Derek appeared, and Anne was full of admiration for Wendy's game. She did not mince her words as she praised her. Roger frowned, but Wendy grinned.

'I can beat Roger most times,' she declared, and he almost winced at her words.

'I'd heard about your game, but I didn't think you were that good,' cut in Derek. 'How do you feel about being beaten by a female, Roger?'

'I'm used to it where Wendy is

135

concerned,' retorted Roger. 'If she hadn't got some strange ideas into her head a couple of weeks ago she would have partnered me over the week-end and I would have won.'

'Does winning mean so much to you?' demanded Anne.

'The competitive spirit is everything. It's a complete waste of time and effort to go out there and not care whether you win or lose. If one is the better player then one should win.'

'It doesn't help one's game to play less than one's best at all times,' added Wendy, chuckling.

'I didn't play to my best because I don't think it's fair that a man should use his superior strength and speed. I tried to remain at your level, Wendy.' There was reproach in Roger's voice.

'That's not how it seemed to me,' Anne broke in, her eyes glinting. 'She had you stretching and over-reaching. You might as well admit it, Roger. Wendy is a better player than you.'

'I like playing with better players. It's

the only way to improve one's game.' Roger sipped his coffee, and Anne pulled a face at Wendy.

'Well, I wanted to see you play and I was impressed, Wendy, but this isn't the place for me.' Anne stood up. 'Come on, Derek, let's find more congenial surroundings. All these athletic types give me the shivers.'

'I agree with you,' said Derek, smiling, and they took their leave.

'Sometimes I find Anne just a little bit annoying,' commented Roger.

'She's only trying to jerk you out of your rather pompous attitude towards life.'

'Pompous? Me, pompous? Do you think I'm a stuffed shirt?'

'Your manner could be mistaken by someone who doesn't know you as well as I do.'

'You know the kind of person I am. I don't care what the others think.'

'But you care what I think?' she asked.

'You've changed over the past two

weeks,' he observed, trying to change the subject.

'Perhaps it is just as well. I expect the rest I had from you did me a lot of good.'

'You don't think I'm good for you?'

'There's a great deal wrong with our relationship, but I have no wish to go into that.'

'I can see that we're not going to settle back into the pattern that existed before you started going out with Alan Scott. I hope he hasn't taught you any bad habits.'

'I found Alan very good company. He certainly knew how to treat a girl.'

'If you found him so attractive then why did you give him up?'

'It wasn't a case of giving him up. I went around with him and discovered that he's not my type.'

'So everything is all right,' Roger said complacently.

She drank her coffee and collected her tennis gear.

'In a hurry to go?' he demanded,

looking up in surprise. They usually sat and talked on almost every subject under the sun.

'You can take me home, but you don't have to leave me. We'll be more comfortable in the flat.'

'But what if Anne and Derek should be there?'

'Anne won't be home until late. Come along.' She started for the door and Roger had to gulp down the rest of his coffee and scrabble up his gear in order to follow her.

He was silent on the drive to the flat and when they arrived he did not switch off the engine. Wendy had almost alighted before she realized that he had not moved.

'Aren't you coming in?' she asked.

'I think I'd better drop into the hospital and see if I'm needed,' he countered. 'They were run off their feet when I left.'

'But you're not on duty and they're adequately covered, aren't they?'

'Yes, but I feel that I ought to go in

and check. You never know.'

'Will you come back afterwards?'

'I don't think so.' He glanced at his watch. 'It's getting late. By the time I return it will almost be time for me to go, anyway.'

'All right.' She stifled her sense of frustration and shrugged. 'See you tomorrow, then. Good night. Thanks for the game. I enjoyed it.'

'Good night, Wendy.' He smiled and when she closed the car door he drove off.

She stood gazing after him, disappointed because she had intended taking the initiative with him, but he must have sensed her determination and cried off for that reason. Sighing, she entered the flat and a sense of restlessness seized her. She did not know if she had made any progress or not, but she could not afford to be impatient. Time was on her side and she had to do everything just right.

* * *

The next morning when she reported for duty, Sister Gilbert departed soon after Wendy assumed charge, and she found herself coping with the every-day problems without her superior's reassuring presence. There were no operations scheduled for the day and the ward was fairly quiet, the work mainly routine. Two patients were discharged and Wendy was pleased when she saw them out of the ward. There was a good deal of chatter among the patients, and handshakes, accompanied by promises to write or keep in touch, then the ward quietened again and order was restored. But the empty beds would soon be filled again with patients coming in for surgery. It would be on Wednesday when new patients were admitted ready for Thursday's operations list, and Wendy sighed with relief as she looked around and discovered that everything was as it should be.

Alan Scott entered the ward around mid-morning, flanked by two housemen. He sent them round to the patients and paused in the doorway of the office where Wendy was checking her paperwork.

'Hello,' he said. 'Hard at it, I see. How is it going?'

'Fine. Everything is under control. This is one of the quiet days.'

'It may be quiet up here, but we've got plenty to do elsewhere.'

'Excuse me, Nurse.' The junior appeared in the doorway behind Alan. 'Mrs. Howard is complaining that she thinks her stitches have pulled loose. She coughed, she said, and she's scared she's done some damage.'

'I'll take a look at her,' said Alan, turning swiftly. 'Show me where she is.'

Wendy accompanied him and drew the curtains around the patient's bed, but it was a false alarm. Alan stood in the middle of the ward and noted the two empty beds.

'Might as well get the round over with,' he said. 'Judging by the notes some more patients will be leaving tomorrow.'

He went to the near end of the ward and Wendy stayed with him, making notes as he chatted with the patients and examined them where necessary. When they had completed the round he sent the housemen off and followed her to the office.

'Any use asking you for a date?'

She looked up at him, her eyes narrowed. 'When?'

'Any evening when you're not playing tennis. Surely the times we spent out together gave you something of a taste for the bright lights.'

'Not really.' She paused. 'I'm not saying that I didn't enjoy myself with you, Alan, but I wouldn't want you to entertain any hopes where none is possible.'

'I don't want to get serious about you. That would be useless. I can see that you and Roger are meant for each other, even if he can't see past the end of his nose, but I need more time to settle in and you can help me pass some lonely evenings.'

'It sounds all right, but you've been here long enough now to be able to put down roots without trouble. I'm not the girl for you, Alan, and you'd only be wasting your time.'

'Thanks for the advice, but I feel that I am the best judge of what's right for me.'

'I agree, but I don't want any further complications. Why don't you try with someone else?'

'Perhaps you're right, but you can't blame a man for trying. I ought to have a few words with Roger and try to straighten him out. He's as blind as a bat and a darned idiot in the bargain. How are you planning to tackle him? I assume that you are going to try and hook him.'

Wendy shook her head and he studied her for a moment before sighing heavily and leaving. She went on with her work and, during the early afternoon, as the visitors began to trickle into the ward, Roger arrived.

'Are you too busy to spare me a few

144

moments?' he asked quietly, glancing around the ward.

'What's on your mind?'

He led her out into the corridor. Wendy tried to read his expression, but his face was impassive, as usual.

'Sorry to drag you away from your beloved patients,' he continued in his gentle tones. 'I've been getting a lecture from Alan and I didn't like it.'

'Did you tell him how you felt about it?'

'You know him. He doesn't listen to anything when he's got something to say.'

'What was the lecture about?'

'You! That's why I'm here. I don't think it is any of his business. He wanted to know what my intentions are towards you.'

'I've been wondering the same thing,' she said, trying to sound casual, but her heartbeats seemed to quicken in anticipation and she clenched her hands.

'I've told you that I love you!'

'You don't have to say it in that

particular tone, do you?' she countered. 'That sort of thing sounds best with soft lights and romantic music.'

'You're being flippant.'

'Life is too short for us to act so serious,' Wendy replied, still smiling, but now there was a firm note in her voice. 'What was your reply to Alan's question?'

'Huh! The cheek of the man! I've already told you how I've planned my immediate future. But tell me, Wendy. If I managed to get this nursing home I want, how would you react to it?'

'I don't follow.'

'It's simple enough. I'll be leaving the hospital and I have my eye on a suitable house close to Broughton. How would you consider an offer to work with me?'

'I think I'd jump at the chance,' she said softly.

'What?' He sounded surprised. 'But how about your career? You're all set to become a Sister. Would you really come with me?'

'I'd follow you to the ends of the

earth if you wanted.'

'This is not a joke.'

'If you can't tell when I'm being serious then there's something wrong with your perception. Anyway, Roger, this is neither the time nor the place to talk about it. I'm going off duty later. What are your plans for this evening?'

'I want to see you. I don't think we should play tennis, so perhaps we ought to have a chat.'

'I'd like that very much. In fact, I'll look forward to it. Will you come round to the flat?'

'Yes. Expect me when I arrive, though. There's no telling when I can get away.'

★　★　★

Later that day a patient was brought in suffering from a broken leg, and Wendy helped the Casualty Officer to rig up traction. Mrs. Church was badly shocked, her face pale, and she was in considerable pain. Her husband was standing in the corridor at the entrance to the ward, having been summoned from work. When the big canvas-webbing belt, with its straps and buckles, had been adjusted, Mrs. Church was given a sedative. The Casualty Officer left, informing Wendy that he would be back later, and Wendy allowed Mr. Church to see his wife for a few moments. She wrote up the patient's chart and then compiled the notes that would be necessary.

When she went off duty she was half-way home before she recalled that Roger was calling to see her that evening. Anticipation began to put a feathery sensation in her heart, and her hands trembled as she let herself into the flat. Was he about to reach a decision? For the first time, Wendy considered the possibility that the decision might be an adverse one for her. Roger might decide that she and his ambitions were not compatible and she worried about it right up until the moment he arrived.

Anne was working until ten that

evening and Wendy sensed the tension in the flat as the doorbell rang. She went in answer and Roger was standing on the step, his expression betraying that his mood was harsh.

'Hello,' he said. 'Am I late?'

'Not at all. Come on in.' She stepped aside and he entered, brushing shoulders with her. She suppressed a shiver and peered out at the warm evening before closing the door. Having made up with meticulous care, she hoped for a compliment from him, but he walked straight into the sitting-room, leaving her to follow.

Wendy could feel a lump rising in her throat. 'You don't seem very happy,' she observed.

'It's Alan. He's been at me several times today. Why can't he mind his own business? It's no concern of his what we do.'

'Oh?' She decided to plunge in. 'Perhaps he doesn't like the sight of me being used as a doormat by you.'

'I don't treat you like that. Don't

embroider the situation, Wendy.' He crossed to the settee and sank into it. 'Come and sit here so we can talk.'

She dropped into the settee at his side, sitting so close that their shoulders touched. She tried to ignore the sensations that surged through her at their contact.

'What's on your mind?' Wendy murmured.

'I'd like you to tell Alan to stay out of our lives. You've finished with him now and he has no right to interfere. We have an understanding and I don't want anything to upset it.'

'Don't you think you're taking all of this just a bit too seriously?' she asked softly. 'Why make all these rules about the way we should exist? So you have ambitions! Don't we all? I've already told you that I'm prepared to give up my ambitions in order to be with you. Do I have to spell it out to you that I love you? You've already admitted to being in love with me — in your own quaint way.'

150

'Quaint?'

'How else could it be described? I don't know what to make of you, Roger. I don't believe you are the type to marry and love and cherish a wife. If you get the nursing home you'll be so taken up with it that you won't have time for a wife.'

'I suppose it must seem like that to you,' he answered slowly, biting his lip, 'but I feel torn between two desires. Apart from trying to get enough money together to launch my project, I do feel the desire to be with you, but romance can only divert my concentration from more important matters.'

Wendy lapsed into silence, aware that no amount of talking would push him into a corner. Roger was not prepared to make a firm decision and she knew she would either have to wait for him to get what he wanted and pray that he would finally turn to her with love and affection or make a decision of her own and finish with him completely. It seemed a good time to make that decision. She was aware of the pros and cons, but there was a limit beyond which she could not go — and he had pushed her to the very edge of her patience.

'I don't seem to be able to get through to you, Roger,' she said quietly. 'We talk, but there's no communication between us. You are going to be preoccupied with your work all of your days. I don't think I can compete against that. If it were another woman it would be a different matter, but this is something I can't fight.'

'I want you, Wendy, believe me, but I can't overcome the compulsion concerning the nursing home. It's been my burning ambition for far too long. All through college and medical training I've had that one object in mind. If you can't accept me for what I am then there's no hope for us.'

'There's certainly no hope for me with the situation as it is,' she retorted. 'I don't think I can go on any longer like this.'

'So what do you suggest?'

'I'm going to seek an appointment at another hospital. I've tried changing friends and that didn't work. Perhaps what I really need is a complete change of scenery. If I get out of your life then perhaps I'll be able to settle down and accept the situation. So what's it to be, Roger? Are we going to have a more normal relationship or do I make the decision to leave?'

The silence that followed seemed heavy and oppressive. Wendy waited passively for a reply, but Roger seemed burdened with indecision and she felt an uncharacteristic impatience seize hold of her.

'For heaven's sake!' she exclaimed. 'Don't tell me we've got to go through all this again. When are you going to make up your mind?'

'You know my mind is already set, but you can't accept it. You want more from me at this moment than I am prepared to give.'

'Very well. I can't go on like this any longer. We'd better part — and for good, Roger. It will be the easiest way out. You go your way and I'll go mine.'

'I'm sorry,' Roger replied gently, 'but that's the way it will have to be. I'll do my best to remain out of contact with you.'

She made no reply, but walked to the window and stood gazing unseeingly at the garden. She heard the door close and knew that it was the second time he had walked out of her life, but with a difference on this occasion — it would be the last time!

★ ★ ★

Next day when Wendy reported for duty she found Sister Gilbert was just about to leave, so Wendy broached the subject that had been niggling her through an almost sleepless night.

'Sister — I'd like to talk to you for a moment,' she said hesitantly.

'Anything wrong?'

'I have a personal problem and it seems that the only way to solve it would be for me to leave the hospital.'

Sister Gilbert looked appalled. 'Oh, grief!' she exclaimed. 'It must be serious for you to quit with so much going for you. Is it something you'd care to talk about?'

'Well, you probably know that I've been more than friendly with Roger Harley.'

'Of course. Everyone knows that one day the two of you will marry. There is speculation, of course, about the length of time you're waiting.'

'That's just the point. We parted a couple of weeks ago to see if it would make any difference to us, but all that it seems to have done is bring the issue into focus and force us to make a decision. Roger won't budge in his attitude, so I can't remain here working in the same hospital with him.'

'I'm truly sorry about this,' said Sister Gilbert. 'You're an above-average nurse and you have a good future here, but if you are not happy then it wouldn't be fair to us to try to influence your decision in any way. I don't think there would be any trouble getting you transferred to another hospital. We could probably do an exchange. There's sure to be a Sister somewhere who would like the opportunity to come to Halesborough. Would you like me to put the matter before Admin?'

'Please. I'm sorry if it is going to cause any inconvenience. After all, I am being trained to take over this ward, but I don't delude myself that I am indispensable.'

'Have you considered all your friends who are here? Won't you miss them?'

'I have thought about it. I spent an almost sleepless night tussling with the problem and I've come to the conclusion that I must get away.'

'All right, I'll put the matter in hand immediately — but I will be sorry to see you go.'

'I don't like the thought of it myself,' replied Wendy, 'but my mind is made up.'

* * *

It was the middle of the morning when Alan Scott arrived in the corridor outside her office — Wendy heard his voice as he greeted one of the nurses. The next moment he entered the office and she looked up at him to see anger in his expression.

'I've just heard the news!' he snapped. 'What's all this about you moving away from the hospital?'

'I — don't know that it is any of your business,' she began hesitantly, but he cut in.

'I made it my business. That was why I egged Roger on yesterday. He said he was seeing you last night. So what happened between you?'

'Why did you take it upon yourself to try your hand at match-making?' Wendy demanded angrily, trying to keep her voice low-pitched. 'You only succeeded in making matters worse.'

'No, I didn't. Matters couldn't be worse for you than they are at present. Roger has no intention of doing anything about your future and you're a complete idiot if you still entertain ideas about him.'

'Well, I'm not a complete idiot and that's why I've decided to go away.'

'Why should it be you who moves? Roger isn't a local man! His home isn't here. Let him move out.'

'I'm not local, either. There are other hospitals in this area which are closer to my home than this one.'

'But you're needed here. They're training you for this job.'

'I'm not indispensable.'

'Neither is Roger.'

'Alan, I appreciate your concern, but it really isn't any of your business,' Wendy pleaded. 'Please forget about it, will you?'

'No, I won't and I have the feeling that you'll be under pressure from other sources before the day is out.'

Wendy transferred her attention to her work. 'You'll have to let me get on,' she told Alan without looking up. 'I have so much to do.'

'I'll see you later, but you'd do well

to rethink this issue. Your decision isn't popular.'

'I'm not concerned about my popularity,' she retorted, and forced herself to concentrate upon her reports. When she looked around a moment later she discovered that he had left.

★ ★ ★

Sister Gilbert returned later to relieve Wendy for her break, and she went down to the dining-room with some misgiving in her heart — and her spirits sank still lower when she was immediately joined by Anne and Marj Blake.

'Don't say anything, please,' Wendy said quickly as Anne opened her mouth to speak. 'I know what you're about to say and I've had enough of that this morning. I'm going to leave Halesborough and I don't want any arguments about the wisdom of my decision.'

'I couldn't believe it when I was told,' Anne replied with a trace of anger in her voice. 'You made up your mind rather quickly, didn't you?'

'It was sudden and unexpected.' Wendy began to eat her meal with great deliberation.

'It's because of Roger! Why the devil can't you forget about him?'

'I can and I will,' Wendy responded calmly.

Anne sighed and an awkward silence reigned while they ate their meal. Then Wendy reported back to the ward and Sister Gilbert broached the subject. Wendy listened in silence, then moistened her lips.

'I know you mean well, Sister, but my mind is made up.'

'I understand how you feel and no doubt I'd act in the same way if I were in your shoes, but I can't help feeling that this is a tragic mistake on your part. I wish there was some other way around the problem.'

'So do I,' said Wendy, shrugging.

She then made a round of the patients and soon learnt that word of her decision to leave had reached their ears. She had to endure the protests and advice they offered, and when she returned to the office it was to find Mr. Holbrook waiting for her. He glared as she paused in the doorway.

'Close the door, Nurse, and sit down,' he commanded and Wendy felt like a naughty schoolgirl up before the headmaster for some minor misdemeanour.

'I have been dragged away from a very good game of golf,' he continued. 'Would you care to tell me what all this nonsense is about?'

'What nonsense, Mr. Holbrook?'

'I received a report that you wish to transfer to another hospital. What's wrong? Don't you like the idea of working with me? Does my manner upset you?'

'It is a personal matter and has nothing to do with my work,' she murmured.

'It may be personal, but it has everything to do with your work. I need you here. I can rely upon you. It eases the burden I have to carry to know that someone like you is up here handling this end of the business. If I am not presuming, would you care to tell me exactly what the trouble is?'

Wendy explained tersely, giving him a general idea of what had occurred, and when she finished he stirred impatiently.

'Why should it be you who moves?' he demanded. 'If Harley plans to leave us when he's in a position to run his nursing home then he may as well leave now.'

'Oh, no!' Wendy shook her head emphatically. 'I'm the one who should go.'

'Not so far as I'm concerned! I want you here and I mean to keep you if I can. Now, continue with your duties and leave this matter in my hands. I'll sort it out.' He paused and there seemed to be a throbbing silence until he spoke again. 'Would you leave with Harley if he asked you to go with him?'

'I think I would.'

'H'm! So it looks as if I would lose

you, anyway! I'm not happy with that. All right, I'll look into it. But you came to Women's Surgical from Geriatric, didn't you?'

'That's right.'

'Do you realize that if you went to a nursing home you'd find that around eighty-five per cent of your patients would be old people?'

'I hadn't thought about it.'

'That's the trend. You'd be back in a job that you hate.' He moved towards the door. 'Think again, Nurse, that's all I ask.'

* * *

At six Wendy went off duty and when she reached the flat she was relieved to find that Anne was not at home. She changed out of her uniform and put on jeans and a sweater. After a meal she tried to relax with a magazine, but had hardly settled when the telephone rang. She went in answer and Roger's voice came over the line.

163

'I tried to get you at the hospital, but just missed you. What on earth are you up to? I've had Holbrook roaring at me. He's been threatening me with every punishment in the book if I don't mend my ways. What have you done?'

'Nothing beyond letting them know of my intention to leave Halesborough,' came the reply. 'I'm sorry you're being troubled, but when I'm gone life will soon return to normal and you won't have anything to bother you except, perhaps, the problem of finding a suitable tennis partner. Now, if you will excuse me, I'll hang up. I have quite a lot to do. Good-bye!'

She replaced the receiver before he could say anything more and went back to the sitting-room. It was too bad if Roger felt that his life was being disrupted, she thought. Who was he to be considered? He had not an ounce of consideration for anyone else. She wondered why she was feeling so aggressive towards him, for she loved him, but it was all one-sided and she was being stung by scorn, for that was what seemed to motivate him.

The doorbell rang and when Wendy opened the door and saw Alan standing there she did not attempt to conceal her irritation.

'Good,' he commented. 'It's about time you got mad. Have you spoken to Roger today?'

'Yes, but I don't want to hear about him. There's been too much said already. I don't know why so much fuss should be made about this business. All I did was ask to be transferred to another hospital.'

'You underrate yourself badly.' He chuckled. 'If anything it will be Roger who is asked to leave so that you can remain.'

'He wouldn't!' Wendy was aghast at the idea.

'Why not? Holbrook has been after him in full cry and you know how much weight he has around the place. If Roger is told to find himself another position then he'll have to do so.'

'But I wouldn't want that to happen!'

'Can we continue this discussion in your sitting-room?'

'I'm trying to have a quiet evening. I've been on my feet all day.'

'I won't keep you standing around,' Alan promised. 'In fact, we can both sit down and chat in comfort.'

'Have you anything constructive to say, or do you want to try to dissuade me from leaving?'

'I'd just like to be in your company. I think you're beautiful and I enjoy being with you — isn't that a change to the usual line you get from Roger?'

'If you mention Roger's name just once more I'll scream!' came the tart rejoinder.

'If that is a condition for entry then I accept and will agree to abide by it.'

She smiled and opened the door wider to admit him.

'You're really in love with him, aren't you?' Alan asked as he sat down.

'You made a promise.'

'I didn't mention his name — but

you are in love with him. Nothing would induce you to look at another man, so I'm not going to try to win you over. However, I have a great deal of feeling for you and I'd like to help. I don't want to see you leave, Wendy, so why don't you try to make him jealous?'

'Listen, if Roger doesn't care enough about me to ask me outright to share his life with him then I won't resort to any kind of trickery to win him. I've had enough, Alan, and that's the plain truth.'

'I'll accept that, but it's only a temporary thing, you know. If you love him as much as I suspect, then, no matter what you do in the short term, you'll have to come back to square one and face reality as it is.'

Wendy stared at him as she took in his words, for she instinctively knew that he was telling the truth. No matter what she did, the fact that she loved Roger remained, implacable and inevitable. She couldn't even run away from it!

6

By the next morning, Wendy had revised her ideas on the situation and, as she and Anne strolled to the hospital, she resolved to put matters right. Anne was nagging her, as she had been doing from the moment they awoke that morning.

'You're wasting your breath, Anne,' Wendy said finally. 'Just leave it be or you'll spoil a perfect friendship.'

'Oh!' Anne was shocked by the abruptness of Wendy's tone and glanced at her, taking in the set expression and the firm lips. 'I'm sorry, Wendy. I know I talk too much, but I have only your best interests at heart. It seems such a shame that you're the one who has to leave. Roger will be going, anyway, when he sets up this nursing home, so why can't you stick it out a bit longer?'

'I can see your point of view and I appreciate your concern, but I've already decided that I can't leave Halesborough. I was feeling sorry for myself yesterday — and being selfish by thinking I could run away from this — but that isn't the answer and I know it.'

They reached the hospital and Wendy went on to Women's Surgical. It would be busy today, she thought, as she entered the office. Sister Gilbert was already there.

'I've been getting it in the neck from Mr. Holbrook,' she said. 'He wants me to put pressure on you to change your mind and stay.'

'Well you don't have to bother, Sister,' replied Wendy. 'I've already decided that leaving won't help me in the least.'

'You mean it?' Relief lit up Sister Gilbert's face. 'Thank heavens! Now Mr. Holbrook will simmer down. I'd better ring him immediately and give him the good news. I wouldn't want him to go into Theatre in a bad mood. He'd take it out on the rest of the staff.'

The pressure of work kept Wendy busy. She attended to the pre-meds and got the patients down to Theatre in good time. The porters tried to joke with her, but she wore a mask of efficiency and kept on working without pause. The first of the patients returned from Theatre and she set up the drip, wrote out the notes and then brought the chart up to date.

The work went smoothly and without fuss and, when Sister Gilbert appeared just before noon, Wendy went along to the dining-room where she was suddenly confronted by Alan.

'So you've come to your senses at last, eh?' he said. 'I couldn't believe it when I heard you'd decided to cancel your request for a transfer. What about an evening out tonight? Put on your best clothes and I'll see to it that you enjoy yourself. I'll pick you up at seven-thirty.'

'Fine. I'll be ready. Now I must hurry — I'm on my break and I have to be back on the ward shortly.'

★   ★   ★

When Wendy entered the flat that evening she found Anne preparing to go out, and her friend was in a cheerful mood.

'What would you say if I told you that I might be getting engaged?' Anne demanded.

'I wouldn't believe it. The way you treat men, I don't think anyone would want you.'

'Well, Derek telephoned a short while ago and the hints he dropped indicate that he's got something on his mind.'

'Is that what you want?' asked Wendy. 'Are you serious about him?'

'I think I am. A girl can't know for sure, can she?'

'There should be a little voice inside you that tells you if it's right or not.'

'Have you ever felt that way about a man? Is that how you feel about Roger?'

'I don't want to talk about him. Any man who places a woman second to ambition wouldn't make a good husband.'

'I'm sorry for you. I've been playing the field for years while you've been very serious over one man, and your world seems to fall apart while mine suddenly slips into place.'

'That's life.' Wendy smiled. 'I'm happy for your sake, Anne. The strange thing is, a girl like me can always lose herself in her work if something goes wrong, while someone like you would be hit really hard if something happened to spoil your plans.'

'That's true. You're the dedicated type. Me, I can take nursing or leave it. Really, I don't think you are the marrying kind, Wendy, and I'm not being unkind when I say that. I think you marry your work, and the same thing applies to Roger. If you both understood and accepted that you'd be better off.'

'I think I have come to understand it!' Wendy nodded thoughtfully. 'But let me know if congratulations are in order for you and Derek, won't you?'

'I certainly shall. There'll be such a party and I'll invite everyone. Now I must get ready. I don't want to keep Derek waiting.'

'Poor Derek! Every time he's called for you he's had to wait. Now you think there might be a ring in it you're anxious to be ready on time. Be careful you don't shock him. He won't be used to you being punctual.'

Anne chuckled and dashed off to her bedroom, and Wendy went into her room to slip out of her uniform. She pulled on a dressing-gown and pushed her feet into slippers, then went into the bathroom to take a shower. She was tired, aching in every muscle, and the hot running water relaxed her and toned up her body.

There was a knock at the door before

she was through and Anne called to her: 'I'm going now, Wendy. Derek has arrived.'

'Good-bye,' Wendy responded. 'Enjoy yourself.'

'I will.' Anne chuckled, and then there was silence.

Wendy smiled wryly as she left the bathroom and went into her bedroom to dress casually. Then she went into the kitchen and made herself a snack. Later she telephoned her mother and had a short chat. She said nothing about the problems that had been facing her and declared that she had no idea when she would get another week-end free.

At that moment the doorbell rang, and Wendy frowned as she said good-bye to her mother and hung up. On her way to the door she remembered the date she had made with Alan and a gasp of shock escaped her as she opened the door to find him standing on the step.

'Hello, what's all this?' he demanded,

taking in her casual garb. 'Don't tell me you forgot about our date!'

'I'm sorry, Alan, but I've had a great deal on my mind. Come in, please. If you won't mind waiting for a moment, I'll make a quick change.'

'No hurry. I'll wait all evening for you.' He entered and closed the door. 'I'll look at the books in the sitting-room while you get ready.'

'What are your plans for this evening?' she called as she went along the hall.

'There's a new nightclub on the outskirts of the town. It sounds like a nice place to spend a few hours.'

'All right. I shan't be long.' Wendy closed her door and hurriedly began to change. She blamed herself for being so forgetful, but her concentration had been on other matters during the whole of the day. She broke all records getting ready, and Alan arose when she entered the sitting-room, a soundless whistle pursing his lips as he looked at her.

'What a transformation!' he exclaimed.

At that moment the telephone rang.

'You're not on stand-by or something, are you?' Alan asked.

'No. Hang on a moment, it could be for Anne.'

Wendy picked up the phone and gave the number.

'Hello, Wendy.' Roger's voice sounded in her ear.

'What do you want?' she asked in a neutral tone.

'I'd like to talk to you. Is it convenient to come round and see you?'

'No, it isn't, actually,' she replied. 'I'm about to go out.'

'Where are you going?'

She was about to retort that it was none of his business, but cut short the impulse. 'Alan is here. We're going out to dinner.'

'Oh! Then I'm sorry for calling.'

'That's all right. Was it anything special?'

'No. Sorry to bother you. Have a

pleasant evening.'

'Thank you.' Before Wendy could say more the line went dead and she frowned as she replaced the receiver.

'Who was that?' demanded Alan from the doorway of the sitting-room. 'Roger?'

'Yes.'

'What did he want — to play tennis?'

'He didn't say, but I wouldn't have been surprised if that was what he wanted.' She smiled cynically. 'Let's go, shall we, before something else crops up?'

He nodded, opened the front door and they departed. Wendy settled herself in his car and resolved that she would enjoy herself. Nothing would be permitted to stand in the way of their pleasure. She was on the threshold of a new way of life and she had to ensure that she enjoyed herself. Only then would the pain of unrequited love be relieved.

Alan was good company and he proved it that evening. Wendy had a wonderful time. The club to which he took her was exclusive, with good food, wine and a cabaret. She was sorry when the time came for them to leave and, when they were in the car on their way back to the flat, Alan reached out and clasped her hand.

'I don't know about you, but I've thoroughly enjoyed myself,' he commented. 'Not once was Roger's name mentioned.'

'You've just spoiled the whole evening,' she retorted, and he chuckled.

'No. Nothing could spoil that now. When you decided against leaving Halesborough you proved that you had broken the hold Roger had on you. You're over the hump now. That's why I asked you out this evening. I want you to get into the habit of enjoying yourself with me. In a couple of weeks, when someone mentions Roger's name, you'll ask who the devil is he?'

She smiled and lapsed into silence, thinking of Roger, but aware that she felt no anguish now, and she was certain that Alan spoke the truth. She had finally worked him out of her system.

When he stopped the car outside the flat, Alan leaned across and kissed her cautiously and Wendy felt herself tighten up inside. But he seemed to understand that she was still not quite her normal self and did not press matters. She thanked him for the evening and he alighted to let her out of the car.

'We must do that more often,' he said quietly. 'I have the feeling that I'm beginning to settle in here now. Good night, Wendy. I'll be in touch with you tomorrow.'

'Good night, Alan, and thanks for such a wonderful time.'

'The pleasure was all mine,' he replied, and waited until she had unlocked the door and crossed the threshold before moving away. Then he departed and when the lights of his car had turned out of the street Wendy closed the door.

* * *

She slept well that night, the pleasure that Alan's company had given her lay like a pleasing mantle over her mind. The alarm clock awoke her next morning and she had to fight against tiredness before she was able to rise. Anne knocked on her door and called in passing and Wendy blinked, stifled a yawn, and got up.

It was as well that today would be rather quiet at the hospital, she thought, and pulled on her dressing-gown. When she went through to the kitchen Anne was already preparing breakfast.

'You look as if you had quite a night,' remarked Anne, glancing at her. 'Hadn't you better start getting ready for duty?'

'What about you?' countered Wendy. 'Did anything dramatic happen last night?'

'About the engagement ring?' Anne smiled. 'We shan't know for a time, I suspect. Derek is being difficult. I've got to meet his parents this week-end, but, reading between the lines, I think I'm home and dry with him.'

'Good. I'm glad for your sake.' Wendy turned to go to the bathroom. 'I only want one piece of toast, please.'

'Where did you go last night? You didn't say you were off on a date.'

'I forgot about it, but Alan asked me out.' Wendy turned on the shower. 'I'll tell you about it on the way to the hospital.'

★ ★ ★

During the morning Alan appeared and Wendy was pleased to see him. He pulled a face as he approached and she wondered if something had gone wrong.

'I was looking forward to taking you out again tonight,' he said ruefully, 'but I'm afraid I've got to stand in for Roger.'

'Stand in for Roger?' Wendy felt an unwelcome tug of emotion inside her and tried to overpower it. 'Is something

181

wrong with him? Is he sick?' She thought of his words the previous evening when he had called her. Supposing he had needed help? She had told him she was going out and he had hung up. Guilt surged through her.

'He isn't sick — it's his aunt. He wanted to tell you last evening when he called, but we were in a hurry. He's been summoned to her bedside. She's in her eighties and it seems the end is near. From what I can make out he's her only living relative and she has pots of money.'

'I know about her,' said Wendy softly. 'I met her once. She was a nice, old-fashioned lady. All Roger's ambitions hinge upon the fortune she will leave him.'

'I wish I had a rich aunt,' Alan said, smiling.

'I wish I could get the time to see her,' Wendy murmured. 'I wonder if that was what he was going to ask me? Perhaps he wanted me to go with him to see her. Oh, heavens, I wish I had listened to him last night!'

'Now don't start worrying about him again.' There was a harsh note in Alan's voice.

'You don't understand. It isn't Roger I'm concerned about, but his aunt. Has he gone off duty? Have you any idea where his aunt is?'

'Don't you know where she lives?'

'Of course, but she may have been taken to a hospital. Is Roger still here?'

'He's over in Geriatric,' said Alan in a grudging tone. 'Can I give him a message for you?'

'Please ask him to contact me before he goes to see his aunt,' she retorted, and such was the note in her voice that Alan grimaced and left.

When Sister Gilbert appeared to relieve Wendy for her break Roger still had not contacted her, and Wendy was filled with indecision. All her instincts were to go to Roger and talk to him, to offer her help in any way possible. The barriers she had erected in her mind against him had crumbled at the first sign of trouble and she knew that if he needed her at all then she would be ready to assist him.

'Sister,' began Wendy, then paused as her superior looked at her.

'Something wrong? You haven't had second thoughts about that transfer, have you?'

'No, it isn't that. I was just wondering — if I needed this afternoon off duty would it be possible to arrange?'

'I expect so. At the moment you can do no wrong.' Sister Gilbert smiled. 'What's on your mind?'

Wendy explained and saw Sister Gilbert nod.

'Yes, I had heard about Dr. Harley's aunt, and I do know that he is leaving very shortly to visit her in hospital. He has quite a way to go. You're very fortunate if you want to accompany him because I am due to have this afternoon off duty, but I'll stand in for you now if you wish to leave. We can always make it right later.'

'Bless you, Sister!' Wendy turned and walked swiftly from the office. She went down to Reception and asked at the desk if Roger had left. When she learnt that he had not yet departed she left a message for him not to leave until after he had contacted her. Then she went to the switchboard and asked the duty operator to page Roger. A few moments later she discovered that he was in Casualty, checking on the last of his daily patients.

Hurrying along the corridors to the rear of the hospital where Casualty was situated, Wendy suddenly met Roger. He was talking to one of the housemen, standing sideways to her, and she paused and studied his profile, sighing heavily as she realized that her love for him would never diminish. That was a fact of life, she thought, waiting for him to leave the houseman, and when he finally turned and saw her he halted in surprise, then quickly came towards her.

'Wendy, what's wrong? You're looking upset.'

'I heard about your aunt, Roger. I was afraid that you'd already gone to see her.'

'I'm on my way now.' His face was haggard, his eyes dull. 'I telephoned last evening to tell you that I'd got word she was ill. I had a further call this morning saying that she had taken a turn for the worse.'

'I'm sorry about last night. I shouldn't have been so curt.'

'Why not?' He smiled gently. 'We are trying to make separate lives for ourselves, aren't we — ?'

'I'd like to go with you, if I may,' Wendy cut in.

He studied her face for a moment. 'Can you get away?'

'Yes. I've already arranged that with Sister Gilbert.'

'I'm ready to leave now.'

'Then I can go with you?'

'Certainly. There's no one I'd rather have than you.'

Roger drove her home and waited while she changed out of her uniform.

Hurrying, Wendy left a note for Anne, informing her friend of her intentions, and then went out to Roger's car.

'Is she in hospital?' she demanded as he took the road that led to Broughton.

'Yes. Not far from your home. Whiteford Cottage Hospital!'

'I know it well. It's a good two-hour run, Roger.'

'Aunt Mabel's home is only twenty miles from your own, if you recall,' he answered.

'That's right. A beautiful little cottage overlooking the moors. I'll never forget that week-end we spent with her there.' Wistfulness crept into her voice and she drew a sharp breath. He remained silent and when she peeped at his profile she saw that he was stern and set, obviously steeling himself for what would most certainly be an ordeal. 'Roger, I don't know if you would rather have come alone,' she said slowly.

'I didn't think! As soon as I heard the news my only thought was to come with you.'

'That's how a friend would react,' he answered softly. 'When I heard last night that she had been taken ill my first thought was to let you know. That's why I telephoned.'

'Don't make me feel any worse than I do already,' she replied. 'I was trying to steel myself against you. That's why I spoke as I did — why my attitude was so harsh.'

'I understand. You don't have to explain.'

They lapsed into silence and Wendy sat motionless, gazing at the road ahead. Roger drove fast but carefully and she knew every inch of the way. She found herself wishing that they could fly. Time passed, and then she looked at him. He was driving automatically, his thoughts probably upon his aunt.

'Did they say she was really ill?' she asked.

'I was told that she is not expected to last through the day. I wanted to get away earlier, but couldn't.'

'That's the worst part of our job,' Wendy observed. 'We're always at the beck and call of duty. Nothing is sacred but the patient.'

'I wouldn't have it any other way.' He glanced at her and smiled. 'Do you want to stop off in Broughton to see your parents?'

'Good grief, no! We'd better go straight to the hospital. I can always see my parents.'

He nodded. 'Still the same old, selfless Wendy,' he commented.

She was tempted to pick him up on that statement, but said nothing, and they drove through Broughton and continued. An hour later they reached the little hospital that was their destination and, as Roger brought the car to a halt, Wendy tried to get her emotions under control.

They alighted from the car and Roger ushered her into the building.

There was a reception desk and she waited while he went to make enquiries. A moment later he came back to her.

'She's still alive, but unconscious. A doctor will come for us in a few moments.'

'Would you prefer to go in and see her alone?' Wendy asked.

'No. I want you with me. We've come this far together.'

She nodded and looked around, taking in the familiar atmosphere of the hospital. It was the same in all hospitals — the cleanliness, the smells, the air of subdued life, as if illness and disease were grappling for supremacy within the walls. This was a very small hospital and the staff establishment not large. They would be a family circle of nurses and doctors, she thought, and wished she could change her place at Halesborough for a job here. She shook her head as she considered that she had applied for such a transfer, but this man at her side was the reason why she could not leave.

She looked at him. He was staring into space, his mind obviously focused upon the condition of his aunt. He was her only relative. She had brought him up after his parents had died, had seen to his education and acted as a mother to him. When she died he would be completely alone in the world and Wendy wondered if such thoughts were occupying him at that moment.

Footsteps sounded on the polished floor and they both looked around to see a tall man in a white coat approaching.

'Dr. Harley?' he demanded. 'I'm Dr. Redfern. I'm so glad you were able to get here.'

'How do you do, Doctor. This is Nurse Curtis, a very close friend of mine.' Roger paused and Wendy heard him swallow. 'How is my aunt?'

'Sinking, I'm afraid. There's nothing we can do for her. If you would come this way I'll show you to her room.'

He turned and retraced his steps and Roger slipped a hand under Wendy's elbow as they followed. They were shown into a single room. The venetian blinds were closed, making the interior gloomy, and Dr. Redfern opened them to admit sunlight.

Wendy looked at the frail occupant in the bed, saw the obvious signs of impending death in the wrinkled, tiny face, and held her breath for a moment as she recalled the only time she had seen this old lady. She wished now that there had been more opportunities. Roger could have visited his aunt more often, but their off-duty time had mainly been spent playing tennis.

Roger paused at the foot of the bed and took up the patient's chart, studying it briefly. Then he glanced at the watchful Dr. Redfern and nodded slowly, as if confirming the situation. He moved around the bed and bent to peer into his aunt's face. The harsh sound of the old lady's breathing was the only noise in the room.

Time passed unmeasured and it seemed like a lifetime to Wendy before

Roger straightened and came to her side, although it was barely more than a few moments.

'She doesn't appear to have much longer,' he said. 'I'll stay at her bedside, but perhaps you would like to have some refreshment, Wendy.'

'If you'd rather be alone then I'll leave,' she answered. 'But if you don't mind, then I'd like to remain.'

Dr. Redfern moved towards the door.

'I'll look in from time to time,' he said, 'but you do understand that I am busy. If you need anything you'll find a nurse close by. Just inform her and she will take care of everything.'

'Thank you.' Roger pulled a chair forward and motioned for Wendy to seat herself. He sat down at the side of the bed and slumped a little, intent upon watching the old lady's face. The silence that enveloped them was tense, oppressive, and Wendy tried to relax.

An hour passed and Wendy became cramped. She arose and went to the window. There was a flower garden outside and a stretch of lawn. Visitors were leaving and she watched them until the last car had departed. Life went on normally, she thought, and was disturbed by Roger coming to her side.

'I really think you ought to go and get something to drink,' he said in an undertone, his head close to hers. 'I won't leave here until she has gone. It could be some time. Perhaps you'd like to telephone your mother and let her know exactly where you are. If this drags on I don't know what we'll do, but I have to be back in Halesborough by morning.'

'I'll do as you suggest.' Wendy glanced towards the figure in the bed. 'I'm glad that I came with you, Roger.'

'Thank you.' He smiled as she turned and left quietly.

There was a public telephone in the corridor and she called her home, getting a reply from her mother. When she had explained the situation, Mrs. Curtis suggested driving over.

'But there's nothing you can do,

Mother,' protested Wendy.

'And if you have to get back to Halesborough without Roger?'

'I'll call again if there are any developments. Otherwise, we'll drop in on our way back. I'm going to get something to eat now.'

'Try to call me later and let us know what's happening,' urged her mother, and Wendy agreed before hanging up.

She left the hospital and went to a café near by. A somewhat stale sandwich and some tepid coffee staved off the pangs of hunger that were attacking her, and then she returned to the hospital. When she entered the small room she discovered, to her surprise, that Roger's aunt was conscious and trying to talk to her nephew. He glanced up at the sound of the door opening, then motioned for Wendy to join him. She walked to the bedside and stood at his shoulder, and tired eyes peered up at her.

'This is Wendy, Aunt. She came with me. She wanted to see you.'

The old lady's head moved almost imperceptibly. Wendy leaned forward and placed a hand upon the gnarled fingers that lay upon the coverlet and her hand was instantly seized in a surprisingly strong grip. The lips moved, but no words issued from the mouth. There were beads of perspiration upon the wrinkled forehead and Roger wiped them away gently.

'Rest easy, Aunt,' he said soothingly. 'We shan't leave your side.'

The old lady's breathing had worsened, thought Wendy, and stroked the hand that clutched at her as if attempting to derive life from their contact. The dark eyes that gazed up at them were unblinking and seemed to be attempting to convey a message. Roger spoke several times in a low tone, asking questions, but received no reply, and, slowly, the breathing eased. Wendy felt the hand gripping hers begin to tighten and Roger reached out and loosened the fingers, smiling gently at her as he motioned for her to move away. A moment later he carried out an examination, then went to the door, Wendy remained motionless while he summoned the doctor, although it was obvious that the patient was dead.

'At least she died peacefully,' said Roger when they had left the room. 'She had a good life, although the past few years must have been very lonely for her. It's too late now to say that I wish I had visited her more when I had the opportunity. There were times when we could have visited her instead of playing tennis so much.'

'Don't blame yourself,' comforted Wendy. 'Life is like that. Each of us has a life to lead and we do what we think is best.'

'What we think is best doesn't necessarily turn out that way, does it?' he commented. 'Go and sit in the car while I make some arrangements with the doctor. Then we'll have to return to Halesborough.'

She nodded and left the hospital, walking in the warm sunlight to his car, and there she stood gazing around, saddened by the death she had witnessed and filled with unanswerable questions. Roger appeared and came to her side. His face was set in harsh lines, his eyes rather bright, and he took her elbow for a moment.

'Thank you for coming, Wendy,' he said. 'This business has brought home to me that a man cannot be entirely alone in this world. I've been selfish and short-sighted. It has taken my aunt's death to prove the point to me. I'm all the things you've said I am and I'll never be able to understand how you've managed to tolerate me all these years. I'm surprised you didn't lose your patience long before you actually did.'

'Shall we drop in at my home on the way back to Halesborough?' she countered.

He shrugged and opened the car door for her. 'You'll come to the funeral with me, won't you?' he asked, and there was a pleading note in his voice.

'Of course.' She nodded as he slid in

behind the wheel, her gaze upon him, and she saw how valiantly he was trying to hold emotion in check. Pity for him welled up inside her and she realized that her love had strengthened because of what had happened. 'You know why I've been so patient with you, don't you?'

'I ought to.' He drove carefully towards the road. 'You've been in love with me for years — and I've been in love with you. We both know that, but I tried to keep my emotions locked away because I thought there were more important things to be done. I don't want to sound mercenary, talking about the situation with Aunt barely dead, but I do inherit a considerable sum of money.'

'I know you haven't been waiting for your aunt to die, but you knew you could do a lot of good with that money.'

She lapsed into silence as he drove towards Broughton. Her own emotions were beginning to overcome the shock that gripped her and she felt tearful.

'I'm not going to buy a nursing home,' Roger then said harshly. 'I've been deluding myself for years. Now I have the opportunity to do what I want I find that it isn't so important after all, but I must add that the realization was striking home before I got the news about Aunt. I've been a fool most of my adult life, Wendy. I've humiliated you, made you suffer unnecessarily, and yet you're still here at my side, ready to help me if I should need it. How can you bear to be in my company after all these years of giving and getting nothing in return?'

'I can only give you the same answer you just had,' she replied softly. 'I love you, Roger.'

'I love you, but my feelings have changed over the past weeks.' His featured were drawn and tired. 'I accept that my love should take precedence over everything else. Are you prepared to give a blind fool another chance, Wendy? Can you ever forgive me for behaving so badly towards you for such a long time?'

She gazed ahead, saw a lay-by, and moistened her lips.

'If you'd care to pull into that lay-by I'll give you my answer,' she said softly.

He glanced at her, then flicked his attention back to his driving, but he slowed the car and pulled into the lay-by. Silence fell between them and he turned towards her. His eyes were still over-bright, but some of the harshness had faded. Yet he did not move, and she guessed that she would have to break the inertia that seemed to grip them. Perhaps he was too ashamed of his past attitude to be able to make the first move.

She reached out her hands and placed them upon his shoulders, then leaned towards him, kissing him lightly upon the lips. He slid his arms about her, drawing her close. When he kissed her it was as if a stranger had slipped into her embrace, a wonderful, passionate stranger whose kisses seemed to set fire to her soul. She closed her eyes, hoping that she was not dreaming. This was what she had prayed for over the long months of the past. His hands stroked her hair and she rested her head against his shoulder.

'I love you, Wendy,' he said in a trembling voice.

She raised her head and looked at him through a shimmer of tears.

'It's not the first time you've told me that,' she replied, 'but it is the first time you've sounded as if you meant it.'

'I do mean it — and I want to prove it. There's nothing else I want in this world but your love.'

'That you already have,' she said. 'It's been yours for as long as I can remember.'

He drew her head down to his shoulder again, kissing her lips and her face, oblivious to the passing traffic that whirled along the road.

'We'd better think of moving on,' she whispered when he paused for breath.

'Time doesn't matter,' he retorted.

'I've got my priorities right at last and I'm going to make the most of them.'

She closed her eyes and relaxed in his embrace. It did not matter that the sun was going down and the first stars of the evening were beginning to make their presence known in the darkening sky. This was where she belonged and where she wanted to be, and now all the signs were that Fate had relented and they were going to find the happiness which had always seemed to be just out of her reach. His urgent lips proved the point and she released her hold upon her control and gave herself up to the promise that beckoned.

We do hope that you have enjoyed reading this large print book.

Did you know that all of our titles are available for purchase?

We publish a wide range of high quality large print books including:
Romances, Mysteries, Classics
General Fiction
Non Fiction and Westerns

Special interest titles available in large print are:
The Little Oxford Dictionary
Music Book, Song Book
Hymn Book, Service Book

Also available from us courtesy of Oxford University Press:
Young Readers' Dictionary
(large print edition)
Young Readers' Thesaurus
(large print edition)

For further information or a free brochure, please contact us at:
Ulverscroft Large Print Books Ltd.,
The Green, Bradgate Road, Anstey,
Leicester, LE7 7FU, England.
Tel: (00 44) **0116 236 4325**
Fax: (00 44) **0116 234 0205**

OFF LIMITS LOVER

Judy Jarvie

Practice nurse Anya Fraser's adopted son is the centre of her busy life. But once her village clinic's handsome new senior partner Dr. Max Calder arrives, he is suddenly in her thoughts more than she's ready to admit. When extreme sports fan Max volunteers to help her with a terrifying charity parachute jump, they grow close. But Anya soon learns that the leap of faith she must take will impact on the home life she's fought so hard to secure.

HUNGRY FOR LOVE

Margaret Mounsdon

When celebrity chef Charlie Irons is let go from his daytime cookery slot, Louise Drew becomes his replacement. But with minimal cookery experience, appalling on-air nerves and disastrous culinary experiments, she is unable to sustain viewing figures and is sacked. She applies for a new job as a personal assistant with catering experience, but realises to her horror that it would mean working for Charlie Irons — and looking after two headstrong young girls. Is Louise up to the task, especially when Charlie's glamorous ex-wife arrives on the scene?

THE MISTRESS OF ROSEHAVEN

Rosemary Sansum

Left widowed and in debt, Rosemary Shaw has no choice but to accept an invitation from an uncle she has never met to come and live at his Rhode Island mansion, Rosehaven. But from the minute she arrives with her young children, she finds the place ominous and unsettling. Even as she begins to fall in love with the mysterious Will Hennessy, it seems that someone is prepared to go to any lengths to prevent Rosemary from becoming the new mistress of Rosehaven . . .

PLAYING MUM

Sarah Purdue

Freya Hardy's sister Astrid has been called for jury service, so she offers to take care of her two nieces and nephew while putting her travelling plans on hold. But Freya soon discovers that being a stand-in mum is much harder than being an auntie . . . Jamie Barnes, deputy head at her nephew's school, is unimpressed with Freya's efforts, and the two of them clash — but when Jamie steps in to help during a crisis, their relationship changes. And when Astrid returns, Freya has a decision to make about her future . . .

NURSE ON SKIS

Phyllis Mallett

Kay is delighted to be back in
Scotland. A new job — district nurse
— is waiting, and her boss is her
uncle, Dr. Edgar Duncan, a GP in
Stranduthie. Excited about her new
life and the challenge of covering
three villages in a remote area, she
quickly settles into a routine. Dr.
Clive Farrell, her uncle's new
partner in the practice, soon falls for
her, and she feels attracted to him as
well. The path of true love runs
smoothly until Dr. Frank Munro
arrives, seemingly intent on ruining
Kay's dream . . .